MIDSUMMER SCHOOL

Midsummer School

David Yaxley

The Larks Press

Published by
The Larks Press
Ordnance Farmhouse, Guist Bottom,
Dereham, Norfolk NR20 5PF

01328 829207

Printed by the Lanceni Press,
Garrood Drive, Fakenham

November 1996

The characters in this book are entirely imaginery and bear no relation to any living person.

ISBN 0948400 49 8

1

'Language, language!' said Roger Barton-Bendish, leaning comfortably back in his seat. 'You're full of strange oaths today. I don't know where you pick 'em up. Well, snap into it, William me lad, we can't stay here all afternoon.'

'What about some help, then?' I asked. 'Hasn't anyone told you the days of the leisured classes are over?'

'Now, be reasonable, old chap,' said Roger, winningly. 'I've got my best suit on.'

'So have I.'

'Yes, but it's not so best as mine. What's the sense of the two of us getting smothered in oil? Besides, I should only get in your way. I'll sit here and cheer you up. Come on, it won't take five minutes.'

It was a waste of time to argue with him, so I bent to my task - bent being a significant word, for the jacking-point of my car, a pre-war Rover Sixteen, was a slot which could only be reached by opening a little trap-door under the driver's seat. As usual, I forgot to tighten the top seal-ring on the hydraulic jack, and at the first stroke about a quart of slimy fluid squirted up my sleeve.

'Dear, dear,' said Roger, as I rubbed it well in with a handkerchief. 'Filtering it for future use? Never mind, pal. These things are sent to try us. Though your empire-made suitings be black, you'll have a better, brighter, whiter soul at the end of it all.'

I got on with changing the wheel. Roger cast a critical eye over the papers for the Summer School.

'Hell of a lot of talent on your course,' he said. 'Listen to this. Mrs. Attlebridge, Miss Florence Babingley, Miss Agatha Bintry, Miss Hester Catton, Miss Erica Cley, Miss Elsie Cockthorpe, Miss Patty Colkirk, Miss Hilda Gissing, Mrs Ada Mulbarton, Miss - hallo! Miss Iris Overy, Miss Gwen Trowse, Miss Meribell Twyford, and the rest. You'll have the time of your life.'

I grunted. 'I don't suppose there'll be one of them under ninety.'

'Too true. Still, there's Iris.'

'Iris?'

'Overy. Met her last year. Teaches at the Borwich High. Hot stuff.'

'I could do with something cool at the moment.'

'Wait till Iris turns the power on. You'll look back on this as a spell in the Arctic.'

We were due at Great Mardle Hall at 4 o'clock, and it was just two minutes past the hour when our front wheels locked on the gravel in front of the main door. We leapt out like a couple of smash-and-grab merchants. The house was an impressive piece of Tudor architecture built about 1850 in a hard, dark-red brick that seemed, unfortunately, to be completely weather-resistant. Framed in the doorway with its four-centred arch stood Dr Norton Subcourse, the one-centred Director of Studies of the University Extension Board.

'Mr Barton-Bendish. Mr Hautbois,' he said, counting us. 'Mm. Yes. We have delayed the - ah - welcoming ceremony. It's always best to be *on time.'*

He had a curious, tricky voice, that rose and sank quite independently of the sense of the words, as if he had an intermittent short-circuit in his larynx.

'Sorry we're late,' I said. 'We -'

'Come and meet the students,' he said, ignoring my bleat. 'They are beginning to get a little restive.' He sounded like some District Commissioner scenting trouble among the natives in the hills of Baluchistan.

We followed him into the house. I was hoping that I could sneak into some convenient washroom, but when he opened the inner door I saw that the tribe of students was before us. There seemed to be about a thousand of them.

'Ah, Mr Gorlestone,' said the Director, as a smallish chief detached himself from the throng. 'Your tutors have arrived at last. May I introduce Mr Barton-Bendish, and this -' he indicated me with a graceful hand - 'is Mr Hautbois.'

We stepped forward simultaneously.

'Dick,' said Mr Gorlestone, puzzling me for a moment. Was it a cabbalistic password, or a mere slip of the dentures?

'Roger,' said Roger, clearing the matter up.

'How d'you do, how d'you do,' said Mr Gorlestone, nodding to each of us.

I never know how to answer this. 'Very well' wouldn't have been true, and 'rotten' would have been tactless.

'I've been looking forward to meeting you, Mr Gorlestone,' said Roger. Liar.

Mr Gorlestone seemed pleased enough. He extended both hands in a gesture of welcome. Roger, being well placed, took the right and shook it. I did the same, mechanically, with the left. Mr Gorlestone beamed at me.

'You're one of us, I see,' he said. 'How long have you been in the movement?'

This was a decidedly awkward question, as I couldn't remember whether it was the scouts or the masons that shook a sinister hand, and anyway I didn't belong to either. I was saved, however, by the Director.

'Mr Barton-Bendish has been delighting us for five years now,' he said. There was, of course, only one movement for him. 'Mr Hautbois has been with us rather less. Rather less,' he added, thoughtfully.

'Ah, yes, but -' began Gorlestone.

'And now we must introduce them to your students, Mr Gorlestone,' said the Director. He turned to the expectant throng. 'Ladies and gentlemen. On behalf of the University Extension Board, I should like to welcome you to this Summer School, arranged jointly by the Board and the Association for the Promotion of Educational Subjects, of which you are all members. Some of you, I know, have journeyed many miles - many miles - to attend this School, and I am sure that all of you are looking forward to some refreshment in the form of tea and, ah, buns. But before we adjourn to the dining-hall, something very important. Something vital, I would say, to the success of this School. You will all have received a name-disc with your papers. Would you now all make sure that you have this disc pinned on your right lapel - your *right* lapel, please - so that we can all get to know each other, and your tutors can make a mental note of your names and faces as we meet. Now, if you would be so kind as to file past us, one by one, we can make our formal acquaintance.'

Too late, I realised that the little disc of cardboard with my name neatly printed on it was not merely some device of the Board's office staff aimed at preventing them from sending the joining instructions to the wrong people. It was now in my waste-paper basket at home.

'Ladies and gentlemen,' said the Director, as the herd began to stir. 'On my left, your tutor for the course on English Literature of the Romantic Period.'

Roger bowed slightly. There was a murmur of appreciation.

'On my right,' continued Dr Subcourse, 'the tutor in charge of the course on Historic Borshire.'

I raised my hands and clasped them above my head. There was a stony silence, broken after a moment or two by a single, quickly-stifled laugh.

No-one seemed in a hurry to meet us face to face, and I had time to tear a page from my diary, print my name on it, and pin it to my lapel. At length Mr Gorlestone set the wagons rolling by bringing up a formidable old girl in black silk. Gorlestone himself was a smallish fellow with an earnest, lined face and thick gold-rimmed glasses, fairly well stricken in years, I thought. But then he introduced the lady as his mother. As soon as she spoke I recognised the influence that had aged him prematurely.

'Mr William Oh-bwah,' she said, peering at my label. 'B.A. Oxford or Cambridge, Mr Oh-bwah?'

'Hobbis,' I said, civilly correcting the pronunciation of my surname.

'Is that one of the newer colleges?'

I let it pass. 'I was at London University,' I said.

'Oh, indeed,' she said, as if I'd told her I was just out of Wormwood Scrubs.

'Well, I shall attend your lectures, Mr Oh-bwah, and I shall be interested to hear what you have to say about our county. I am, of course, a native of Borshire. I hope you will be punctual. People notice, you know.'

She had another look at my label, gave me a curious, distasteful look, and extended a paw. I shook it, transferring the top layer of grime from my palm to hers. She passed on to Roger with a pale, set face.

Apart from that, the whole business was vaguely depressing. I had expected that the mean age of the students would be fairly high, but some of the hands extended towards me were so frail that I had a momentary expectation of being left holding a fistful of wizened fingers. Those who weren't old and wrinkled were old and large. Late in the procession, however, came a few bright spots. First there was Sandra Litcham, a tall, slim librarian with elegant legs and a small, husky voice full of vague promise. She was followed by a few sixth-formers from Borwich High School, led by their English mistress, Miss Iris Overy, a lush brunette with a figure that left little to be desired. Or a lot, to put it another way. They were the last persons to present themselves to us, and I was thankful that most of the dirt had been removed from my working hand before I took Miss Overy's.

'I'm very pleased to meet you,' I said, repeating the formula, but this time meaning it.

'Hello. Roger has told me so much about you,' she murmured.

'Oh, ah?' I said. That was another opening to which I had no sensible answer.

'I'm hoping to find out whether it's all true,' she continued, hanging on to my hand. 'I'm sure it's not possible for any man to be such a paragon.'

'Odd you should use that word,' I said, trying to create a diversion, for the sixth-formers were all within interested earshot. 'Until I looked it up the other day I had an idea it was a bird of some sort.'

'And what is it?' asked one of the girls.

'Oh, a person or thing of supreme excellence. But it can also mean a mate or consort in marriage. Most peculiar,' I added, hastily, as they giggled. 'Not a bird at all.'

'I think we shall have to watch you,' said Miss Overy. 'It wouldn't do for you to be a paragon to us all, would it? Would you care to read my label?' she said, thrusting it towards me. 'I'm afraid it's not nearly as interesting as yours.'

'Miss Iris Overy,' I murmured. I couldn't help noticing that it was pinned extremely close to the edge of the neckline of her blouse. In fact, it seemed to be in some danger of falling into a cleft which, as far as I could discover without actually peering down, was more or less bottomless. 'I hope to see more of you,' I added.

She gave me a look expressive of agreement, and passed on. I felt somewhat happier. One swallow doesn't make a summer, it's true, but Miss Overy seemed likely to provide some leavening in the indigestible lump of my students. I scanned the labels of the sixth-formers with renewed interest, but I didn't recognise any of the names as those that appeared on my list. It was as I'd feared: Roger had got them all. They were an attractive lot, too, particularly the last of the line, a bright hazel-blonde in a dappled, tawny dress that was reminiscent of a medieval tunic. I read her label.

'Miss Katherine Southwood, B.A. Good Lord!' I said. 'I'm sorry. It was just that I thought you were - well, one of the girls. Perhaps I'm getting old. Or else it's the contrast with the rest of the students.'

She smiled. She had the sort of delicate, creamy skin that makes your finger-tips tingle, and the smile produced a pair of dimples. A real *peach.*

'Mr William Hautbois, B.A.,' she said, reading my label. She pronounced my name correctly, but rather spoiled the effect by giggling.

'What's the joke?' I asked.

'Oh, it's not your name,' she said, apologetically, 'it's just that the rest of the information is - well, unusual.'

I detached my label and studied it. It was a blank page torn from the diary sent to me with the compliments of Snorehill & Wheatacre, Agricultural Merchants and Suppliers of Animal Foodstuffs and necessaries, and now read:-

January 21
Wednesday
First quarter
MR WILLIAM HAUTBOIS, B.A.
see page 15 for table of gestation periods

Tea, to which we adjourned, exhausted by handshaking, was uneventful. I found myself at a table with four elderly ladies. Two of them were engaged in a muttered conversation about their legs, and the rest of us weren't invited to join in. The third returned random answers to the two or three remarks that I offered. I decided that she must be either stone-deaf or a gentle nutter. The fourth, a tall, scrawny old girl, was preoccupied with eating. She evidently hadn't had a square meal since early in the century, and was now determined to make up for it: sandwiches, sausage rolls, bread and butter, jam, cakes, tea in gallons, all vanished in a flash. In the absence of anything better, it was quite entertaining. I was somewhat relieved, however, to find that she and her three companions were hell-bent for Eng. Lit. of the Romantic Period, and not Historic Borshire.

The interval between tea and supper was for settling in. I collected my luggage from the car and consulted the typed list of room allocations. The house appeared to have several floors and innumerable bedrooms, among which male and female were scattered at random. The authorities must have been either innocent ('I'm afraid I don't quite see what you're driving at'), trustful ('After all, Enderby, they're responsible adults'), cynical ('Putting them on different floors won't alter their sex') or simply fed up ('Oh, to hell with it, Fred, bung 'em all together'). Or perhaps they merely thought we were all past it. Anyway, I found my allotted room at the second attempt, and had time to unpack before the gong went for supper. I managed to avoid the Frightful Four of tea, and squeezed in between Dick Gorlestone and the hazel-blonde girl, who was now wearing what appeared to be a pair of flowered pyjama trousers under her tunic. Opposite us were Mrs Gorlestone, Dr Bawdeswell, and Iris Overy. Roger, I noted, had got Sandra Litcham and the sixth-formers at his table. Marking down his prey, I supposed.

The conversation was not exactly sparkling in the opening stages. Someone mentioned the weather, which was hot, and hoped it would last. The rest of us agreed. Then, doing my duty, I asked Dick Gorlestone about his Association, and was answered at length by his mother, who had, apparently been in at the foundation in 1853 or thereabouts, and had known every leading person in the movement from A. B. Apton to Hamilton Wormegay.

'Our interests are boundless. Boundless,' said this good lady, making a boundless gesture with her claw. 'Religion, politics, history, the arts, foreign affairs, the empire, social questions, science, education, civilisation itself. It is our humble boast that nothing - *nothing* - is too difficult or too advanced for the APES to study.'

'The apes?' I asked, startled.

'The Association for the Promotion of Educational Subjects. Our little joke,' she explained, with a sort of spasm of the upper lip that I recognised, by sheer intuition, as a smile. 'We have our lighter side, Mr Oh-bwah.'

'Hobbis,' I corrected her.

'Oh, but it's far more than a hobby,' she said, severely. 'For some of us, APES is a way of life. I hope that before the Summer School has ended we shall have convinced you of the seriousness of our concern for liberal studies, at least. Indeed, I hope to make some converts among the students, for not all' - she lowered her voice and glanced about her - 'not all are members. We are forced, by economic factors, to accept applications from outsiders, and I am afraid that there may be some here whose concern for learning in its widest sense - *in its widest sense* - is minimal.'

'Perhaps so,' I said, not wanting to commit myself either way. I suspected that anyone under the age of fifty was *persona non grata* with the APES.

'Young people today,' she went on, nosing the air, 'are not serious. What, for instance, are these young gels here for? Merely to get a little more information to cram into their examination answers. And what is the end of the examinations? Do they lead to a lifelong interest in liberal studies? No! All they lead to is a position as a typist in an insurance office. An insurance office,' she repeated. It was, she implied, the main depôt for the white slave trade. 'Then, in a year or two, they get married.'

'Don't you believe in marriage, Mrs Gorlestone?' asked Iris Overy.

'Certainly I believe in marriage. It is a woman's duty to get married and bear children,' she said, with Edwardian forthrightness. 'But marriage should not stifle. I was married for twenty-three years and bore three children, but I was not stifled.'

'Pity,' murmured the hazel-blonde.

Mrs Gorlestone looked at her sharply. Evidently there was nothing wrong with her hearing.

'Aristotle held,' I said, hoping to avoid bloodshed, 'that the ideal ages for marriage were thirty-seven for a man and eighteen for a woman.'

'Are you not married, Mr Oh-bwah?' asked Mrs Gorlestone.

'No. I can hardly support myself, let alone a wife.'

'Have you no occupation?'

'Oh, I'm fully occupied. Never an idle moment. There's this sort of thing - lectures and what-not, mainly in the winter, of course. And then there's my career as an unsuccessful writer.'

'A writer? What do you write, Mr Oh-bwah?'

'Novels.'

'Oh, novels,' she said, examining her plate of sponge pudding and custard with some suspicion. 'I never read novels. I have far too much to do.'

'I practically *live* on them,' said Iris Overy enthusiastically, with a nice undulation of the neck to show how supple they made her. 'What kind of novels do you write?'

'Historical.'

'I should have thought that kind of thing is very popular,' said the hazel-blonde girl. 'Practically every novel in the public library is bursting at the seams with how nows and gadzookses and my lord of Essexes.'

'Too true,' I said, gloomily. 'If you happen to write about the gadzooks period, as I do, it's gadzooks or nothing. Eschew gadzookses, and you're lost.'

I spoke feelingly, having had two novels, both of which I'd considered strikingly different from and superior to the ordinary run of historical fiction, refused by a total of twenty-seven publishers.

'And is this lecturing all the *work* you do?' asked Mrs Gorlestone, when I'd had my say about the slit-trench that historical-novel readers had dug themselves into.

'Oh, there's other odd bits and pieces. Indexing - articles for the local papers - ancestor-hunting for the Mormons. I'm a kind of historical scavenger, really. And then I've got a couple of barns full of mushrooms that have to be coddled and tucked up in bed and so on.'

'Mushrooms?' said the Southwood girl. 'My father grows mushrooms.'

'Does he?' I said. Perhaps that's where I'd heard the name before.

'You're quite a jack of all trades, Mr Hautbois,' said Dr Bawdeswell. We all knew the rest of the phrase.

'The bedrooms here are very nice,' said Iris Overy, turning the conversation with surprising tact. 'Which floor are you on, William?'

'It's odd you should ask that,' I said quickly, slightly embarrassed at her use of my Christian name. 'Looking at the list of room allocations, I thought the authorities had been very liberal-minded, mixing us all up together, male and female, but stap me! I wasn't quite prepared to find a pink nightdress, all frills and ribbons, laid out on the bed of the room I'd been given.'

'A present from the gods,' said Dr Bawdeswell.

'A typing error, not a moral one,' I said. 'Disappointing.'

'Whose nightdress was it?' asked Iris.

'I didn't ask. Probably some frightful old girl of ninety-five.'

'Which room was it?'

'Well, I'm in room D, floor three, now. The room with the nightdress was room B on the same floor.'

'Room B is my room,' said Mrs Gorlestone.

The hazel-blonde girl choked on her coffee, sending a good half-pint over my trousers. I made the most of this small diversion by patting her on the back and mopping up; then, muttering that I'd have to go and change, I left the table.

That evening the Gorlestones were laying on an Educational Entertainment. Roger and I held a brief conference on events and prospects in his room.

'Not too bad as yet. I saw you chatting up four of your birds at tea,' he said. 'Be careful, Willy me lad, some of those old girls can be hot stuff. The long thin one had a distinct gleam in her eye.'

'Worms,' I said. 'If I'd been almond-flavoured with a dollop of cream on top I wouldn't have stood a chance. Anyway, they're not my birds, they're yours.'

He let out a howl.

'What, all of 'em? Do you mean to say I've got to sweat my guts out selling the Romantics to that lot?'

'Shouldn't be difficult. They were probably personal friends of Wordsworth. Anyhow, besides the human boa-constrictor, there's the pair that's only interested in their poor old legs, and the fourth is stone deaf. It's a sinecure. And you've got all those sixth-formers.'

His eyes lit up.

'True. And there's a gorgeous librarian. Name of Sandra Litcham.'

'The one with the low voice?'

'What an uncouth way of putting it. It's a lovely voice. Hidden depths -'

'Perhaps it hasn't broken properly yet.'

'Have you no soul? No, I suppose you haven't. Well, how are you doing with Iris? Nice girl. Highly recommended.'

'If you're so keen to sing her praises, how come you've not planted the Barton-Bendish colours on her peak? Peaks, rather.'

'Oh, well, this and that. You know how it is,' he said.

'Oh, yes,' I said, not knowing at all. 'Well, to change the subject, what do you reckon to the floor-show tonight?'

'William, old lad,' he said, 'I fear the worst.'

I suppose, technically, it could have turned out worse. The film projector could have broken down, and then we'd have been left with the Gorlestones unrelieved. But it was bad enough. 'Wild Wales: a Medley of Sound and Vision' they called it. There was a slide projector, a movie-projector, and a tape-recorder. The pictures, as pictures, weren't bad, but one always had the feeling that the wrong technique was being used. The milling crowds of a market and the pageantry of an Eisteddfod were on colour slides, while we had minutes (or so it seemed) of shots of the distant Snowdon, Yr Eiffl, and Cader Idris on the film camera. The tape recorder churned out fragments from the works of Beethoven, Elgar, and Ivor Novello. And there was the commentary, spoken - and on one occasion sung - by Mrs Gorlestone: gems from the early rhapsodists and the Victorian tourists, and poems in the Welsh - at least the general assumption was that they were in the Welsh, although there was a small school of thought at the back of the room which held that at these moments the tape recorder was running backwards. And besides hogging the spoken word, Mrs Gorlestone couldn't keep off the screen, either. Beth-Gelert was dominated by Mrs Gorlestone in belted raincoat and sou'wester. She stalked among the ruins of the abbey of Vale Crucis in heavy tweeds, thick stockings, and a highland bonnet. She rose through the spray of Pistyll Rhæadr to obliterate the waterfall. Enveloped in an enormous ulster, she stood on a cowering outcrop of rock and pointed an accusing finger at an insignificant lump on the horizon while the tape-recorder thundered out that peculiar Welsh poem on Snowdon that consists entirely of vowels and the letter R. Wild Wales struggled gamely against the Gorlestone attack, but it was on a loser all the way.

Roger and I, being officially off duty, got as far back in the room as we could. Roger was in the middle of his sixth-formers, while I had Iris Overy on one side and Miss Hester Catton, a thin old character with a lined, bristly face, on the other. As soon as the lights went out Miss Catton went to sleep. This in itself wouldn't have mattered but for the fact that her head kept rolling against me with a peculiar, rubbery action, and every time I pushed it back to a more-or-less upright position it emitted a loud snort. The attention this attracted was particularly undesirable as on the other side Iris's hand had clasped mine early in the proceedings, and the light from the projectors, though flickering, was certainly enough for any eye but the dimmest to see what was going on.

'I trust you enjoyed the show?' said Dr Bawdeswell, leaning forward to speak to me after the lights had gone up. He was sitting on the other side of Iris, but he hadn't got either a squeeze or a whisper out of her.

'Very interesting,' I said, cautiously. I didn't trust him.

'Ah,' he said, glancing down. I withdrew my hand hastily from Iris's warm fingers, and automatically gave Miss Catton a push. She was, unfortunately, awake.

'Oh, sorry,' I said, as she bristled at me. 'Wretched fly. Well, it's hot drinks, then bed, I suppose.'

'Ah, bed, lovely bed,' said Iris.

'Which floor are you on, Miss Overy?' asked Dr Bawdeswell.

'The third.'

'Ah, then we'll all be together,' he said, with a smile that, whatever the intention, appeared full of lechery.

'How nice,' she said, without enthusiasm. 'Katherine dear, shall we go and get the kettle on? There's a little kitchen-thing at the end of the corridor on our floor. I expect the men would like something hot.'

We said we would. I had to stay behind to congratulate the Gorlestones on their performance, and the little kitchen was crowded when I finally got there. Several genuine APES were concocting preservatives, Iris and Sandra Litcham had been cornered by Bawdeswell and Cyril Thrigby, and Katherine Southwood and a medium-sized chap with a confident voice, fawn trouserings, and a kaleidoscopic designer sweater labelled Tony Saham were dispensing tea and cocoa.

'Tea, please,' I said, in answer to the girl Southwood's enquiry. I pushed past Stan Hoe, champion cocoa-drinker of north Bradford, and took the cup from her. 'Thank you. And thanks, also, for the coffee at supper. I had a good half-cupful when I wrung my trousers out.'

'I'm dreadfully sorry about that,' she said. 'Were they very wet? I see you're wearing another pair.'

'We tutors have to observe the conventions. Anyway, it was a useful diversion at the time.'

'I just couldn't help it.'

'I thought you'd done it a-purpose. Well, what with that and the earlier remark about stifling, I'll bet your name won't be inscribed in the lady's book of gold. Did you enjoy the show tonight?'

'Frankly,' said Tony Saham, with a confidential turn of the head, 'I thought it was a load of crap. Thank God we were in the back row. I hope the rest of it isn't going to be as grotty as that.'

While agreeing in principle with this view of Wild Wales, I felt I ought to stick up for the teaching and admin. side, so I said that as a matter of fact I'd quite enjoyed it.

'Yes, so we noticed,' said the girl. 'Tea or cocoa, Mrs Gorlestone?' she added, as the leader of the APES appeared in the doorway.

The Gorlestones, we gathered, were not to partake of the common muck that the rest of us were corroding our guts with. They had their own peculiar brew, and their insistence on piling into the kitchen and taking over the kettle necessitated some rearrangement among the occupants. Tony Saham found himself pinned to a distant wall by Elsie Cockthorpe, and the girl Southwood and I were crushed pleasantly together against the broom cupboard by the enormous rear parts of Mrs Winch.

'I don't think they trusted me to make their tea,' said the girl. 'Personally, if I were that woman, I'd even have my toothwater analysed.'

'No doubt she uses her son as a taster,' I suggested. 'I'll tell you if he drinks before she does. Ah, there he goes. The first sip. Note the lifted eyebrow, the pursed lips, the ball-cock in the throat. Then the pause; the contorted face; the strangled cry, the clutch at the stomach; the convulsions of the body, and the last fall into the pit. Ah, well, you can't win them all.'

The girl's giggle unfortunately coincided with a pause in the general hubbub. Mrs Gorlestone turned and gave us a long look. It wasn't difficult to see the way her mind was working.

'You can see the way her mind's working,' I said, when the noise had begun again. 'The satyr in tutor's clothing - the innocent, unsuspecting maiden - late drinks - unseemly propinquity. I can see I'll be up before the Court of High Commission before the week's over. I suppose I can plead that I was the victim of circumstances.'

'I'm not sure I like that,' said the girl. 'By the way, that's my cup of tea you've just finished.'

'Oh, sorry. I thought it tasted extraordinarily nice. Would you care for some of mine?'

'No, thank you,' she said, smiling.

'Very wise. If Mrs G. saw us drinking from each other's cups she'd fear the worst.'

'I shouldn't think she fears anything.'

'What are you two whispering about?' asked Iris, squeezing past Mrs Winch's elephantine backside. 'My goodness, I thought I was never going to get away from those two old goats. Katherine dear, why don't you go and rescue Tony? That Cockthorpe woman looks as if she's going to eat him alive.'

'Like the female spider and her mate,' said the girl.

'My dear, how horribly zoological!' said Iris, with a pretty shudder. 'We never got past the rabbits when I was at school. So interesting, their little habits. Poor boy! He looks positively mesmerised. Do go and rescue him.'

'Oh, all right,' said the girl, rather grudgingly, I thought. 'But I'm not going to fight her for him. If I don't come back you'll know I've been trodden on and squashed.'

She eased herself past Mrs Winch.

'A sweet girl,' said Iris, thoughtfully.

A few minutes later the curfew sounded, in the form of an announcement from Mrs Gorlestone that as we had a heavy programme on the morrow it was time we all went to bed. There was only one bathroom on our floor, she continued, and we must see that we were all decently clothed when moving to and from the said place. The corridor light would be left on all night. She trusted to our good sense to ensure that there would be no vulgarity or horseplay. She advised the ladies to lock their doors. Then she stalked out of the kitchen and into the bathroom. The rest of us drifted into the corridor and formed a rough queue while we were still decently dressed. In a couple of minutes there was a familiar clank and the rush of water descending from a great height.

'I declare this loo officially open,' muttered Katherine Southwood.

I clapped politely. Mrs Gorlestone, emerging, divided an extremely suspicious look between us and took up her station immediately opposite the bathroom. She stayed there until the last person had finished.

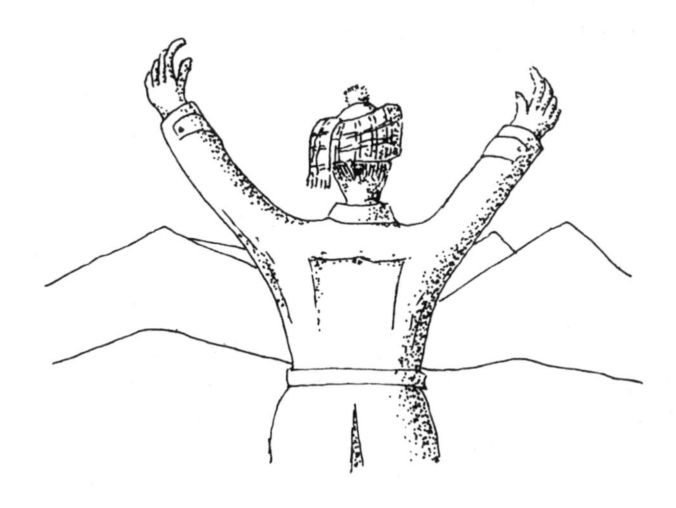

Wild Wales

2

My normal breakfast - a small loofah of cereal and a round of toast - is eaten in a solitary, morose silence, the head bowed down over some improving book, and I grudged having to break this simple and decent habit. The old folk, apart from two who were lying in bed with their stomachs, seemed determined to prove that they were still alive after the long dark night. They were full of sprightly chatter and unseasonable questions. What was that large tree in the park? Would we be going to see any old Baptist chapels? Did I know that the great-nephew of Nelson's valet lived in Borshire? Was it going to rain? Miss Patty Colkirk, an ebullient heavyweight from Eastbourne, asked my opinion of her theory, formed on a recent coach-tour of the Highlands, that the Scottish kilt was a direct descendant of the Roman *tunica.* All I could think of was a feeble jest about Macgillicuddy's Breeks. Roger, I noted sourly, had briefed his sixth-formers to keep him a place at their table, and whatever they were talking about I was pretty sure it wasn't Baptist chapels or Nelson's valet. The only lightening of the gloom came when the portly Mrs Ada Mulbarton stepped backwards off the slight platform on which our tables were placed and took with her in one majestic swoop Mrs Queenie Winch and a third monster, Hilda Gissing, with a tremendous display of drawers and trunk-like thighs. All three had to be towed back to their rooms. With the two stomachs, this meant five less for Historic Borshire. At this rate, I thought, I'll be talking to myself by the end of the week.

The main event of the morning was the combined debate, 'Whither Education?' As I had no official role I found a quiet armchair at the back of the room with a good view of Iris Overy's legs and let them get on with it. My abstention did not go unnoticed.

'Mr Hautbois,' said Dr Subcourse, handling his mid-morning biscuit in a delicate, scholarly way, as if it had been produced by the university archivist, 'did you enjoy our debate this morning? So many important issues were raised, one scarcely knew which way to turn. So *important,* don't you think, to get people talking early in the course? But they must be led by the *professionals,* if I might so term the, ah, tutors.'

'Sly old groin-kicker,' I said to Roger, when the Director had taken his cup and biscuit elsewhere. 'I suppose he thinks I'm not earning my fee. Well, that was an APES debate, pure and simple. I'm Historic Borshire. I'm damned if

I'm going to squander what little energy I have on Education, its Disease and Cure.'

'Is this wise?'

'Very. The moment I opened my mouth you'd have seen there was nothing in it. Incidentally, you spouted a hell of a lot of guff. Good guff, of course. The jargon came out like sausages out of a top-hat. Very public-spirited.'

'Wheels within wheels, old son,' said Roger, confidentially. 'It was for the doctor's benefit. My whole future depends on the impression I make on him this week.'

'The new job, you mean? Resident Officer of the University Extension Board?'

'Exactly. You interested?'

'Had a letter yesterday. I'm on the short list.'

'You too? There's three of us here - me, you, and Tony Saham. Ye gods! I'll bet old Subcourse has planned it like one of Stephen Potter's House Parties at the College of Lifemanship. Wonder if our bedrooms are bugged?'

'That'd limit your activities.'

'No problem. I'm the strong, silent type.'

'Yes, but what about the other half? Better avoid it, B.B. One squeak of female ecstasy and your whole career's down the drain. Who's Saham, anyhow?'

'The yuppie in the snazzy sweater. You were talking to him and his popsie last night.'

'Yes, I know who he is, but not *who* he is.'

'Doing a spot for me later on in the week, on the Romantics and the theatre. Postgraduate at Borwich, doing seminal work on the cultural life of regency Borwich. Brilliant, so he tells me. His dad's the pro-vice-chancellor.'

'Spot of nepotism imminent, you reckon?'

'Shouldn't be surprised. All's fair in love and education. No, no, what am I saying! Of course, with Subcourse at the helm, everything's bound to be fair and above board, and all that. I don't think. Well, here comes one of your young ladies. Cheerio for now, and be good.' He sloped off.

'Ah, Mr Hautbois. I've been talking to Mrs Gorlestone about the kilt,' began Miss Colkirk, 'and do you know, she thinks...'

I began to wonder how long it was to lunch.

'Sunday is such a bad day for visiting cathedrals,' said Iris to the company at dinner that night. 'I think we might let the clergy have it to themselves for that day of the week, at least. It's so uncomfortable for the trippers to find themselves *embroiled* in religion, when all they want is to gawp at the tombs. And one never sees the dean.'

'You saw several canons this afternoon,' I said.

'That's not the same thing at all. There's nothing exotic about them. Canons are all rosy and porty, or else practically mummified. Deans are thin and ascetic and full of hidden passions. There's something devilish about deans.'

'It's their legs,' I suggested.

'My father was Dean of Borwich,' said Mrs Gorlestone.

That, of course, was the end of that conversation.

'What are we to have tonight?' asked Dr Bawdeswell. 'Ah, yes. "Beautiful Borshire", by Mrs - ah, yes. Delightful. You seem to be getting off pretty lightly,' he said, turning to me.

'Oh, but William took us over the cathedral this afternoon,' said Iris. She was sitting opposite Dr Bawdeswell, and now she bent forward, giving him a glimpse of Happy Valley. 'Don't be so demanding, doctor. I'm sure you'll be satisfied by the end of the week. Won't he, William?'

'He might,' I said, cautiously. It depended on what he wanted.

'Are we having some more of your marvellous pictures tonight, Mrs Gorlestone?' he asked.

'There will be both Sound and Vision,' said Mrs Gorlestone.

'So biblical,' murmured Iris.

Borshire being a flattish county, it didn't provide the same opposition to Mrs Gorlestone as Wild Wales, and the contest was a walkover. The Borshire landscape could do little more than peep coyly round the fringe of the Gorlestone tweeds or shrink away from her outstretched arm. No tension. It was rather as if King Lear had risen to defy the elements and had then found that it was, in fact, rather a mild evening.

There wasn't much doing in the audience, either, at least not in my part of it. I was stuck between Dr Subcourse and Cyril Thrigby. Mrs Gorlestone had put a curse on smoking, so the doctor spent the entire session extracting delicate little grunts and whiffles from an empty pipe. Cyril Thrigby went into some sort of trance.

'Most enjoyable,' said the Director, when at last the lights were turned up. 'An admirable introduction to a week of what one *hopes* will be serious study. A high standard for you to follow, Mr Hautbois. I shall look forward to seeing how you tackle the subject.'

An unpleasant thought struck me.

'Will you be here all the week?' I asked.

'M'mm. Oh, yes, I shall be here. Here and there. I shall be here. Oh, yes,' he said, packing the bowl of his pipe, 'I shall be here. Not with you all the time, of course. I'm very keen on the Romantics. Very keen. You won't mind if I just drop in when I can, will you?'

The answer that sprang readily to the lips, of course, was 'Yes', but this might have been impolitic, so I smiled a wan smile and said I would be delighted. I supposed he was getting some incredible screw for seeing that we did our jobs, so the least he could do would be to drop in. There was always the chance that if he dropped hard enough he might sprain something.

'William, old lad,' said Roger, edging in as the Director went off to pay his respects to the Gorlestones, 'what time is it? My watch has got the staggers.'

'Half past nine. Our curfew goes about ten.'

'The Gorlestone? Oh, well, there's lots to be said in favour of an early night. Depends who you're sharing it with, of course. Anything going in your kitchen?'

'Hot drinks. Served by your tall, dark husk.'

'Sandra? Lead me to it.'

He led, of course. The kitchen was crowded, but Roger eased himself in and inside a minute he and Sandra Flitcham were in a distant corner, clasping mugs of cocoa. Her defection from the brewery meant that I was temporarily drinkless, and I was in the middle of boiling a kettle when the Gorlestones arrived, thirsting for theirs. They commandeered my water, and in exchange offered me a cup of their tea. Over it, Mrs Gorlestone became confidential.

'I am a little worried about these young gels,' she said. 'In my opinion the rooms have been allocated very stupidly. The sexes have been mingled with no discrimination whatsoever. I spoke to the bursar about it, but he was most uncooperative. I cannot see that it is healthy to have young gels in such close proximity to men of all ages. I fear pranks, Mr Oh-bwah.'

'I expect they've been told to behave themselves.'

'But there are the men, Mr Oh-bwah. Who is to rule them? And there is no discipline nowadays. The example of the mistresses...'

'Quis custodiet ipsos custodes?'

'Precisely. If I observe misconduct or horseplay by any person - any person whatsoever, Mr Oh-bwah - I shall do my duty.'

'Oh, yes?' I said doubtfully, and took a sip from my cup.

'Do you not care for our tea?' she asked, seeing, I suppose, some twitch of the mask.

'Oh - er - well, I expect it's something in the water.'

'It is our own mixture,' she said, coldly. 'Calamint, the leaves of the holly, and burdock.'

'Good for the juices, and some other things, ha ha ha!' said Dick Gorlestone. 'But not quite the old camp-fire brew, hey? Oh, hello, Miss Overy. May I offer you a cup?'

'Oh, Mr Gorlestone, thank you, I'm absolutely gasping for it,' said Iris, appearing in the doorway. She took the proferred cup. I should like to have seen her face when she took the first gulp, but she had her back to me.

Meanwhile, there was my cup of hellbrew to be disposed of. I moved quietly out into the corridor. Katherine Southwood and Tony Saham were snugged in a little niche by the stairhead. They had the air of two persons about to do something interesting.

'It's like the Black Hole in there,' I said, approaching delicately. 'Much cooler out here.'

'Oh, yes?' said Saham, with a twitch of the mouth that I interpreted as a minimal smile.

'On the other hand, the tea's in there.'

'We were just coming in for it,' said the girl.

'Ah. Er - I've - er just had a warning from the Camp Commandant, and I thought I'd better tell you. She fears pranks. Sex, in other words. Thou shalt not do anything. At least, not in public. I thought I'd better warn you. You look as if you ... here, would you like some tea?' I added, hastily, seeing that Saham, for one, was about to advise me to go and see a good taxidermist. 'I've hardly touched it.'

He refused, rather shortly.

'Thank you, I would,' said the girl.

'No, I shouldn't if I were you,' I said. 'It's the Gorlestone special. Calico, leaves of the holly, and bird droppings. I'll get rid of it.'

I'd just disposed of it round the S-bend when Roger and Sandra Litcham came out of the kitchen.

'William, old boy,' said Roger, clasping me on the shoulder, 'Sandra and I are going for a little stroll in the garden, to get rid of the fug. Close, isn't it? The front door's only got a yale lock on it till eleven. Slip down and put it on the latch in about half-an-hour's time, there's a good chap.'

'Oh, all right,' I said, resignedly. 'Half-an-hour?'

'On the dot. I'd leave it on the latch myself, but some old busybody would be sure to come along and lock it. Thanks, old chap. Do the same for you, of course, should the occasion ever arise.'

They slipped away, just missing the start of Mrs Gorlestone's state visit to the loo. There didn't seem to be much for me to hang about for, so I retired to my room. The air was certainly a bit muggy, and I threw open the window to get the benefit of whatever spicy breezes were going. It was pretty dark outside, and there were flashes of lightning and a few belly-growls of thunder somewhere over the back of the house. Not the ideal weather for a nuzzle in the garden, but Roger would find a sheltered nook somewhere, and anyhow the storm might not be over us for half-an-hour. So I settled down with *Barchester Towers*, and I suppose I didn't notice how near the tempest was getting until, about five minutes before I was due to go down and unlock the door, there was a tremendous flash, a head-splitting crash, and all the lights went out.

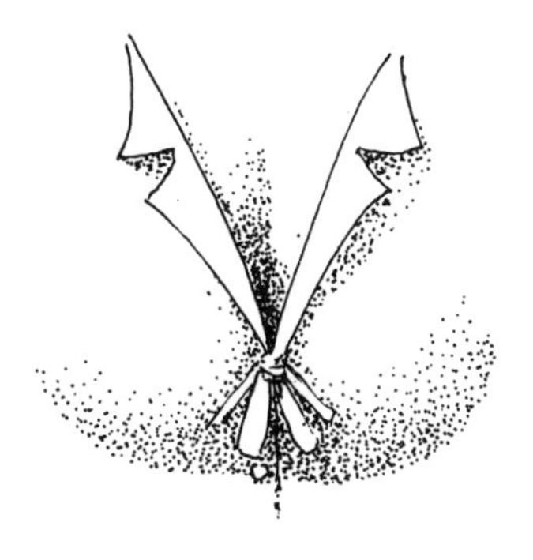

Happy valley

3

It would, perhaps, be an exaggeration to say that on the failure of the lights all Hell broke loose in Great Mardle Hall, but certainly a dickens of a lot of miscellaneous noise rose up and beat about the darkened mansion. The logical reaction to an Act of God is, I suppose, to sit still, but no-one seemed inclined to be logical, and after a little while I felt a bit left out of it. So I felt my way to the door and opened it.

I got the impression that there was a fair amount of something going on in the corridor, but as it was pitch black I couldn't see exactly what. Bumpings, squawkings, whisperings, and an occasional querulous 'what's happened?' from some of the dimmer folk filled the air. Mrs Gorlestone, however, rose to the occasion.

'Ladies and gentlemen!' she trumpeted. 'There has been an electrical failure.'

There were actually a few murmurs of genuine surprise.

'We must keep calm,' she continued. 'You must all return to your rooms. There is no need for alarm. The company's workmen will do all that is necessary to repair the fault.'

We were, on the whole, a pretty docile lot, and the sound of shutting doors showed that she had, at least, prevented a stampede or a riot. There seemed to be rather more panic on the floor beneath us, where most of the sixth-formers were lodged, and there were signs that there was at least one opportunist among the men there, for amidst the giggling and squeaking I could distinguish remarks like 'what do you think you're doing?' and 'keep your hands to yourself'. Mrs Gorlestone distinguished them also.

'Richard!' she bawled.

'Yes, mother?'

'Go down to the next floor and tell those young persons to get back to their rooms.'

'But I'm in my pyjamas!'

I couldn't see that it mattered, unless, of course, the lights should come on while he was down there. But Mrs Gorlestone evidently thought the risk was too great.

'Mr Oh-bwah!' she called.

By the time I got down to the second floor most of the hubbub had died down, but there were still a few young gels to be sent back to bed and one or two old dotties who needed assurance that we were not in the preliminary stages of Doomsday. By the time I'd finished the lightning had given way to solid rain, and the house was as black as the pit. It wasn't all that easy to locate the stairs, but once I was on them the ascent was fairly simple - at least, it would have been if, half-way up, I hadn't suddenly remembered my promise to Roger to unlatch the door. With a stifled oath I turned sharply about, forgetting that the stair was highly polished. The heel skidded, the legs flailed, and some strange reflex action of the thews and sinews launched me into space.

Quite a number of people, from Satan to Peter Pan, have enjoyed the sensation of free flight, but I didn't think much of it. Perhaps my trip was too short, although at the time it seemed to last a couple of hours. I flew through the air in silence, but I touched down with all the delicacy of a ton of Derby Brights and, skidding along the landing, knocked some occasional piece of furniture, a table or chair, down the next flight of stairs. It made the most frightful clatter, and as I lay there, wondering whether the neck was broken, I expected doors to open by the dozen and the hubbub to break out afresh. In fact, there wasn't a single enquiry. Perhaps the old folk, if they heard it at all, thought it was some mad frolic of the young people, and no doubt the young people, philosophically, dismissed it as just another of the old dodderers breaking a leg or something, what the hell. So I was forced to pick myself up. A quick check established that, although shaken, I was unfractured, and after a pause to get my bearings I recommenced the ascent, this time, however, on my hands and knees. Needless to say, I'd forgotten all about Roger. I reached the top landing without further incident, and turned along the corridor. It was hellish black and smelt of floor polish, and the only way to find my room was to count the doors. My bedroom was the fourth along.

Where I went wrong was in forgetting that the kitchen came before the bedrooms. Looking back, I see this lapse as one of those quirks of fate that would have made Thomas Hardy spit on his hands and reach for the quill. If only I'd remembered this detail all the fearful brouhaha of the next few days would never have arisen; but I didn't remember, and when I touched the fourth door I had no thought but that I was on the threshold of my little grey home in the west. I found the handle, turned it, and pushed the door open.

There wasn't much to choose between the blackness of the corridor and the blackness of the bedroom. The bedroom ought, in theory, to have been a shade or two lighter, but in practice I could perceive no difference. I closed the door behind me and moved forward. Almost at once I collided with a chair. By clinging together we managed to avoid falling, but something was dislodged, for I heard a broken smack and a kind of scuttering sound. I couldn't think what it could be, so I bent down and swept my hand over the floor. The lino was awash. I hadn't time to work out what this might mean, for at the second cast my fingers closed on what a moment's consideration told me was a fine set of teeth.

Later in the week, when I'd had to endure a few dozen slings and arrows, I would, no doubt, have passed this off with a shrug of the shoulders and a wry smile; but as yet I was completely unhardened, and I don't mind admitting that I hit the ceiling, or as near as dammit. Once the first shock had passed, however, I calmed down. For one thing, there'd been no reaction at all from the owner of the teeth, and for another, a second or two's reasoning told me that they could not, in fact, be enmouthed, but were lying, naked and unashamed, on the floor. They must, therefore, be removable, that is, false. I had erred in supposing that I had entered the Hautbois chamber. I was standing in another's room. I must lose no time in getting out.

My first attempt at an exit told me why the rightful owner of the teeth had made no complaint about my intrusion. I stumbled on to the bed, and found it was empty. This was a relief, for I'd been half afraid that there might be an elderly lady there, cowering under the bedclothes and expecting a fate worse than death. I found the door at last, and lost no time in slipping out. Once in the corridor, I leant against the wall and tried to work out where I'd gone wrong. I was reasonably sure that my counting was right, and it wasn't long before I remembered the kitchen. If I'd counted the kitchen door as a bedroom, I'd only progressed three true bedrooms down the corridor instead of four. Whose room was next to mine? I couldn't remember. Anyway, that was what had happened, no doubt. The next door along would be mine.

I began to edge along the wall, and was doing quite well in a modest way when I became aware that I was being followed. Something down by my feet was making a kind of frittering, prickly sound. A *hedgehog?* It couldn't be, not on the third floor. I was about to lash out when my hand touched the next door, and simultaneously a muffled roar came from the end of the corridor. Someone had just pulled the chain and would be coming out, perhaps with a torch. It was but the work of a moment to find the handle, turn it, and nip through the doorway. Peacehaven! I heaved a great sigh, and feeling in need of a little rest put my hand out to where I reckoned the bed ought to be. It came to rest on a face.

For the second time in five minutes I leapt skyward, but this time I wasn't given an opportunity to calm down, for the whole damned bed seemed to rise up. The air was filled with bedclothes, pillows, and small, painful blunt instruments. A sharp stab in the groin doubled me up and a bang in the eye straightened me out again, and as I staggered away some blankety thing descended over me. It was the very deuce to get rid of. There seemed to be several square miles of it. I might have been there yet if I hadn't trodden on the edge and overbalanced, coming down in a heap on top of my opponent.

Pausing only to add a handy pillow and what felt like a candlewick bedspread to the pile, I was away. For once the lap of the gods was pointing in the right direction and I found the door-handle almost immediately. I'd slipped into the room pretty quickly, but that was like a slow-motion replay compared with the way I went out. Some irresistible force slammed the door from the other side, and I heard the key turn in the lock.

Well, that was that. At least I was cutting down the possibilities. I leant against the locked door to get my breath back, but after a few draws I realised that this wasn't the best place to convalesce, so I turned to the right and took a tentative step, or rather tried to: my foot wouldn't budge. Paralysed! A vital nerve severed! But then I wiggled my hips, and discovered that the bottom of my right trouser-leg was jammed in the door.

It was one of those crucial moments. The whole of the past life of those trousers seemed to pass before me, right from the time that I'd bought them as a FANTASTIC REDUCTION to their present unfortunate predicament. Finding that mere leg-movement wouldn't free them, I bent down impulsively to get more hand-purchase. Victims of some internal mechanical stress, they split straight up the seat. Undaunted, I crouched and pulled; but for all the joy I got that worsted and polyester mixture could have been screwed to the woodwork. And the door was locked.

Once again I had to stiffen the sinews of the brain and sort out alternatives, and once again, thanks to a Liberal Education, they came.

1. Bang on the door until the inmate opened up or I broke it down. Either way the whole floor would be roused and my plight made public. Not attractive.

2. Cut the leg off. The trouser-leg, you fools. Heartbreaking for the trousers, of course, but otherwise sensible. Unfortunately I hadn't got a knife with me. Leg not readily accessible to teeth.

3. Take my trousers off.

One of the songs I learnt at my father's knee was a lament beginning 'I didn't like the trousers I was wearing, so in the street I took them off, you see'. The air of sad but logical inevitability about this sequence had always impressed me, and no doubt it now took a big part in the councils of my subconscious. Anyway, the more I thought of my present situation, the more it seemed the only course. Once debagged, I could nip into my room, grab a knife, and with simple, surgical precision cut the corner off the leg, leaving a mere unidentifiable tuft jammed in the door.

Once the decision was made I was out of the trousers in a flash, and was actually moving away when I remembered that I still hadn't located my room. I'd tried the fourth and fifth doors, with poor results. Where the hell was chez Hautbois? I toyed for a moment with the idea that I was on the wrong floor, but that wouldn't do. I could remember coming up the stairs. But this thought gave me pause. In the darkness one stair is much like another; suppose I'd come up the flight at the *other* end of the corridor? The more I thought of it, the more plausible it seemed. If I'd come up the wrong staircase, I'd have been on the wrong side of the corridor. No wonder I'd gone into the wrong rooms! All I had to do now was to go to the other end of the corridor, find the stairhead, count four - no, five, to allow for the kitchen - five doors along, and there I'd be, home at last.

I went. I found the stairhead, and counted the doors. By the time I got to the fifth the mood of optimism had vanished. I couldn't be sure that I was on the right side of the corridor, or even that the corridor was on the right floor. There was no telling what those miscellaneous bangs on the head had done for me. I might have wandered for miles.

I hesitated for at least a minute, but at last desperation took over and I turned the handle. The room, I need hardly say, was as black as a midnight hag. I pushed the door open. It creaked a little, and I waited for the yell; but nothing came, so I ventured a little further. I had to go quite a long way before I touched anything, but at length I found the edge of a table, and on the table was a book.

Odd how the human mind works. There was no earthly reason why I should have assumed that I was the only person in the house to possess a book, but as soon as I touched it I knew I was in my own room. Moreover, I was as certain as dammit that the book was Cobbett's *Rural Rides,* vol. i. It had the coarse, grainy feel of Cobbett. I picked it up - with some vague notion, I suppose, of smelling it, since I certainly couldn't see it - and of course I dropped the thing. The next moment I was bathing in light.

Well, paddling might be a better word, as the torch-beam lost no time in travelling down to my trouserless legs. It dwelt on them for an indecent period while I stood there pretending, in a paralytic sort of way, that I didn't belong to them. There didn't seem to be anything very appropriate to say, particularly as I didn't know who was behind the torch. As the beam moved upward again I instinctively put out my hand to shade my eyes. This gave me an idea, and in a moment I had both arms outstretched in the classic sleepwalking position. I turned to the door, and was about to pass through it when the torchbearer spoke.

'William!' she said.

It was Iris Overy.

I ought to have kept on walking, like Felix. But I was so relieved to find that it wasn't someone like Mrs Gorlestone that I stopped and turned.

'It's all right, William,' she said. 'It's only me.'

I regained my voice. 'I'm terribly sorry,' I began, 'but I lost my way in the dark, and I thought this was my room -'

'How disappointing! I really thought...' Her beam wandered down to my legs again. 'Do you often wander about without your trousers?'

'It's a long story,' I said, hastily. 'I think I'd better -'

'You're not going yet, surely?'

'Well, I really think -'

'You can come in for a little bit, surely. Come in and shut the door. That's right.'

I came in and shut the door.

'Now you can tell me all about it,' she continued. Her torch flitted over the furniture. 'I'm afraid I'm terribly untidy. The only place to sit is the bed. You don't mind, do you? I'm quite decent.'

Well, of course, standards of decency vary. Compared with the Cnidian Venus she was well wrapped up, and the average nudist would have considered her overdressed. She had turned the torch beam away from me and on to the bed, and a good deal of light fell on herself. Her hair was long enough to reach her shoulders, but between its lowest tendrils and the frill of her nightwear there was an appreciable expanse of Iris unadorned. She did, indeed, make an attempt to haul the bedclothes up, but it was only a gesture and achieved little except to display the silkiness of her arms. I sat down on the bed, pretty stirred up.

'Tell me all about it,' she murmured.

I told her most of it, in a rather distracted way.

'Poor William!' she said, when I'd finished. 'What a night! And are you all right after that fall?'

'I think so,' I said, feeling the old nut rather gingerly. 'I'm not quite sure where I hit it, and anyway the virago in the other bedroom gave me a wallop in the eye.'

'Let me see,' she said.

She put the torch down on the bedside table. I leant forward. She leant forward. The bedclothes slid away a little. She stretched out her arms to me, rising out of the lacework. She put a hand on my forehead.

'How's that?' she whispered.

'Gorgeous,' I murmured.

She clipped her hands round my neck and lay back on the pillow. I followed her down, perforce, and sailed smack into one hell of a kiss, warm, soft, and smoothly tongued. For a while our mouths stuck together like the two halves of a mussel shell, but all too soon we had to surface for air, and it was during this breather that a thought struck me with a sudden and most inconvenient sharpness.

'Hell's bells!' I cried. 'Roger!'

'Where?' she said, sitting up with a jerk.

'Outside in the rain. I was on my way to let him in when all that business began.'

'Oh, you gave me such a fright,' she said, reproachfully. 'Not very tactful, William dear.'

'Sorry. I don't know what made me think of him. In the circumstances.'

The circumstances certainly seemed to be working against Roger's best interests. I don't know whether it was our joint exertions or her sudden start, but one of the straps of her nightdress had slipped and a damask bud was peeping over the frill.

'Let's forget Roger,' I said.

But you know how it is. I felt like the man who was told he would find a fabulous buried treasure at a certain spot, provided he didn't think of a white crocodile while digging. Even as my fingers wandered over the satiny curve of her shoulder, the vision of Roger and his girl standing outside in the rain rose waveringly before me. At the next breather I explained it all. I must say Iris took it well, even lending me a pair of nail scissors and her torch to retrieve my trousers. All in vain. There was neither hide nor hair of a trouser in sight in the corridor. Bewildered, I popped back to tell her. She took it calmly.

'I expect they'll turn up,' she said. 'You've got another pair for tomorrow? Well, don't worry about them tonight, William darling. It won't take you more than a minute to get down to the door and back, will it? Borrow my dressing-gown. It's in the wardrobe.'

If my brain hadn't been put temporarily out of joint by all the events of the night I would have found my own room with the help of the torch and safely trousered my legs. However, I was still in a bit of a daze, so I went to the wardrobe and put on the dressing-gown like a child. It was a long quilted affair, and left only the ankles showing.

'Don't be long, William dear,' said Iris.

We had a brief, passionate embrace, and I set out on my travels again. This time I could move much faster, thanks to the torch, and I must have come close to the record for descending the stairs to the main hall. The door was not yet bolted, and it would have been the easiest thing in the world just to have turned up the latch and nipped back upstairs. The thought came to me, however, that Roger and his girl might well be sheltering in the porch, so I opened the door and peered out. I couldn't see them, but it was a large porch, about the size of a four-bedroomed semi-detached, with a few nooks and crannies, and to make sure I took a few steps out and scanned the far corners. Apart from a brush, a basket, three old Wellington boots, and something that looked like an ancient scalp, there was nothing there, and I was just turning to go back when I heard a soft click.

I knew what had happened before I tried the door. For a few moments, I confess, I stood there in despair, clunked to the marrow by this latest blow, but gradually the numbness ebbed and the brain began to wriggle again. After some painful grinding I decided that the only thing to do was to try to find some other way in, for any alternative meant that I would almost certainly have to reveal myself in Iris's dressing-gown to strange, and possibly critical, eyes.

So I joined the hosts of Midian and prowled around. I was banking on there being a window open somewhere, but there wasn't. Not a crack. The house was as dark and secure as a mausoleum. Unhealthy, I thought it, all those airless rooms, breeding germs and dry rot in the stale air. By the end of the week we'd probably all be down with yellow fever or the sweating sickness. How people could go frowsting on, stewing in their own breath, beat me; far better to be striding through the clean night air, soaked to the skin and glorying in the naked elements. But after a couple of circuits of the house I felt that I was in some danger of becoming a fresh air addict. One must, of course, have moderation in all things. So I began to look for a window to force, something well away from the inhabited quarters. Eventually I found what I wanted, a small casement through which I could make out some sort of obscure back kitchen, which looked as if it hadn't been used since the third scullery-maid hanged herself there in 1883.

There are certain basic tools that anyone who is going in for housebreaking, even as a hobby or occasional pastime, ought to have, and I hadn't any of them. A swift search of the area revealed nothing that would be of any help in forcing the window open, and it became evident that I'd have to break a pane and release the catch from inside. I found a hefty chunk of brick, and with this in my hand I nerved myself for the deed of shame.

In fact, the first few blows were so timid that I didn't even crack the pane, but a particularly heavy flurry of rain made me desperate, and the next whack was a winner all the way. I hadn't expected the glass to break with muffled boots, but the actual noise took me aback. It seemed, to my quivering ear, rather as if some careless giant had put his foot through the roof of the Crystal Palace. I cowered against the wall, awaiting the inevitable hullabaloo; but when a couple of minutes had passed and I'd heard nothing I took courage again and opened the window - not an easy job, by the way, as the catch was arthritic and the hinges almost completely seized up. However, I got it open enough to let me squeeze through, and I was tiptoeing through the scullery, bent low to avoid swinging corpses.

I won't detail the rest of that night's wanderings. I hadn't the faintest notion of the relationship of the scullery to the dormitory wing, but I reasoned that, as the scullery was a semi-basement room and my chamber was on the third floor I couldn't go wrong if I kept going up. I abandoned this theory after I'd spent some time in the attics. It seemed hours before I found myself in the main hall. After that it was just a matter of going up the stairs, but when I got to the familiar corridor I was faced with the old problem: which was the Hautbois Room? Fortunately the dying breaths of the torch gave me the clue to the error of my former ways. The villain was the kitchen, which had not one but two doors, the second unused but possessing the handle and door-like attributes that had thrown my calculations out. If my room was the fourth bedroom on the kitchen side, which I was pretty sure it was, then I must count six doors. I did - three times, and on the third opened the door. The torch was no more than a glow-worm by this time, but it was enough. Home sweet home! Beautiful!

Whether it was more beautiful than what awaited me in Iris's room was conjectural. But I wasn't sure that she'd welcome me with open arms. I'd been away a hell of a time, and her dressing-gown looked like something salvaged from a second-class dustcart. Moreover, I was as tired as yesterday's lettuce, and by the time I'd stripped off my wet clothes, hung them up, and dried myself, I was just about dropping off to sleep. I wouldn't, I felt, have been able to do her justice. So I went to bed.

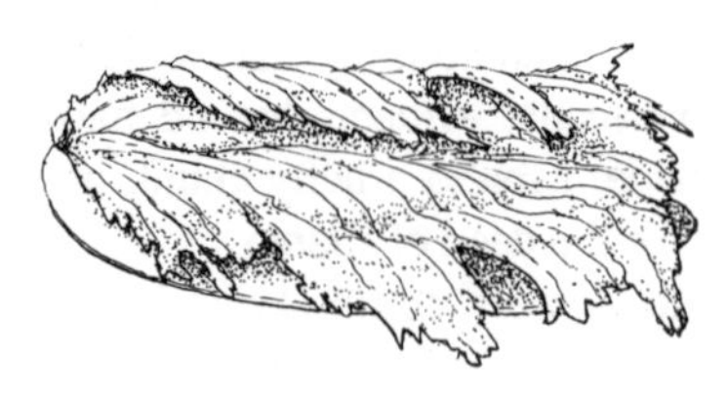

Yesterday's lettuce

4

Next morning a sodden dressing-gown, wet clothes, the absence of a pair of much-loved trousers, and, when I came to look in the mirror, a thumping black eye, convinced me that the alarming events of last night had been real and not just a dream. I ran through the grisly catalogue while I was shaving, and in the course of this the disposition of the rooms, which last night had escaped me, came back. I worked it out half-a-dozen times, but I couldn't get away from the conclusion that the first room I'd raided had been Mrs Gorlestone's. My stomach turned over at the thought of what might have happened if she'd not been at the loo when I called. Hell's bells! As it was, she could hardly fail to discover that there'd been an intruder, what with the scattered teeth and so on. The only consolation was that it wasn't her door that had snapped up my trousers, but the next one, that is Katherine Southwood's. And what had happened to the trousers? Would they be produced as Exhibit A? The black eye, too, might be suggestive. It was, presumably, a present from the girl Southwood - unless she'd had someone in with her when I entered, which might account for the absence of the customary halt-who-goes-there routine. If, in fact, she hadn't been alone, she might well decide to keep quiet about the whole affair; but this was a slender hope, and I went down to breakfast in a mood of apprehension.

I got a lot of sympathy for my black eye, most people seeming to accept without question my story that I'd fallen downstairs in the blackout, which was, of course, true. I kept away from the rest of the *dramatis personæ* of last night's production, but I couldn't avoid a couple of meaning glances from Iris. What they actually meant, however, I couldn't tell.

My first lecture of the course was on the subject of the Puttocks, a Borshire family that by thrift, marriage, guile, fraud, jobbery, venality, barratry, and every kind of legalistic skulduggery had conned its way to vast possessions during the Wars of the Roses, only to fritter them away in a gentle decline to aristocracy during the next two centuries. The lecture itself went down fairly well, the only flies in the ointment being Dr Bawdeswell, who attacked me with a steady stream of questions and comments designed to prove that he knew much more about the subject than I did, and Mrs Gorlestone, who lived near Caddow Castle, the chief residence of the Puttocks in the sixteenth century, and thought this entitled her to belong to the family. On the other hand, Katherine Southwood came to my assistance on a couple of occasions when Dr Bawdeswell had been particularly bloody-minded. I couldn't understand what she was doing at the lecture at all, as she was pricked in the list for the Romantics, but there she was, and her intervention was very welcome. At half-past ten we finally laid down the cudgels, and after a hasty coffee the whole party boarded the coach that was to take us on our first excursion.

'I really think I must have been a swallow,' said Miss Patty Colkirk, leaning most of her fourteen stones against the railing at the top of the tower of Caddow Castle.

Ten solid minutes of her conversation had left me pretty numb, but I suppose my features, working like the legs of a hen when the head has been chopped off, registered some surprise, for she added:

'In another existence, I mean.'

'Oh, yes?' I said.

'Such graceful birds, aren't they? How the spirit flies with them! Do you know, Mr Hautbois, I almost believe that if I cast myself over the edge I would skim away on the wings of the wind.'

I nodded. It seemed to me more likely that she would do a tremendous belly-flop into the moat, but I didn't want to say anything that would deter her from trying it. She held back, however.

'One can truly get the feel of the past in places like this,' she went on. 'When I think that in this very tower - in the very chamber beneath us - poor sweet Margery Puttock languished from love of her - er - boyfriend - oh, Mr Hautbois, my heart is wrung. Wrung! And yet she was free in spirit. Free as thistledown, free as the birds of the air. Stone walls do not a prison make -'

'These are brick, actually.'

'- nor iron bars a cage. Have you read Meg MacTintavy's *The Laird of Buttanben*, Mr Hautbois? Oh, it's a most moving book, and so much history in it. It's about a young Scottish heir...'

I let my mind wander a bit while she ran through the plot. I'd promised to stay at the top of the tower until all the party had been up. Miss Colkirk and I had been alone for some minutes now, but I was pretty sure that there were more than a dozen of the party who hadn't come yet. Still, it was a climb of ninety-odd feet, so perhaps some of the more senile hadn't made it. In fact, I had a suspicion that two or three had sneaked back to the coach after their first glimpse of the tower and were now stuffing themselves with sandwiches and

Swiss roll. I hoped, without caring very much either way, that they'd been savaged by the coach-driver, a palæolithic thing in oily pin-stripe who, but for the fact that he'd had to cling to the steering wheel, would have rent me limb from limb for making him bring his lovely fifty-seater along such bloody little god-forsaken ratgullets of roads, as he put it. It was at this pleasing point that I became aware that Miss Colkirk had paused, as if for comment or an answer.

'I'm so sorry, I didn't quite catch that,' I said, bending an ear.

'I merely remarked, "Ah, the souls of those that die, are but sunbeams lifted higher".'

I don't know what sort of response she expected to that one, but my polite grunt was unfortunate, for she took it to mean that I still hadn't heard what she'd said. She repeated it, isolating each word. This made it even more paralysing.

'H'm, sunbeams,' I said, musingly. 'Sunbeams.' And then something drifted across the blankness of my mind. 'Extracted from cucumbers?'

From the hard, spiritual look she gave me I gathered that the association hadn't been a happy one. Perhaps she didn't like Swift. Or cucumbers. Anyway, she beetled off down the mouth of the spiral staircase, leaving me alone.

Not for long, however. I was just thinking I ought to go down and see what had become of the rest of the party when there was a clatter of footsteps and the girl Katherine Southwood appeared.

'Oh, there you are,' she said. 'I bring you good tidings of great joy. Mrs Mulbarton is stuck on the stairs.'

'Oh, yes?'

'Mrs Gorlestone sent me to find you. The body's blocking the way up. And down, for that matter.'

'What does she expect me to do? Rig up a pair of sheer-legs?'

'Perhaps she needs your *moral* support.'

There was a slight amount of leg-spin on 'moral', but I didn't want to go into all that now. Anyway, at that moment Mrs Gorlestone's voice, inquiring if any-one knew where Mr Oh-bwah was, came whizzing out of the doorway, having gained a considerable muzzle-velocity from the spiral stair.

'There you are,' said the girl. 'I bet she knows where you are.'

'Tell her I went down another way. Oh, hell, all right, I'll go. It'll soon be time for dinner, anyway. Have you seen the rest of the party? Miss Overy, for instance?'

'The last time I saw her she was with Slimy Joe.'

'Who?'

'Sorry, Dr Bawdeswell.'

'Oh. Thank you very much, by the way, for your help this morning. I can't make out what you were doing at the lecture, though. Or here, for that matter. I thought you were down for the romantics?'

'Oh, I did a swap. There she blows again.'

Mrs Gorlestone's voice, now definitely impatient, boomed in the shaft.

'So she does. You wouldn't like to go and tell her that I'm not here, I suppose?'

'No, I wouldn't. Forward, the Light Brigade!'

'Who, me?'

'You're paid for it.'

'Heartless wretch,' I said, stepping down the hatch.

'Heartless, perhaps, but not trouserless,' she said, remaining firmly behind.

It took us about half-an-hour to get the giant Mrs Mulbarton down. I once helped to bring a grand piano down from a third-floor flat, and this was very much the same sort of operation, the similarity even extending to a repetition of the traumatic experience of having my guts jammed against the wall by a damn great bulbous leg. However, at last she was free, and I was able to secure my sandwiches and fling myself down on the sward to enjoy them.

'It's wet,' warned Dr Bawdeswell. Just too late, of course. The overnight rain went through the seat of my trousers like an X-ray. I got up.

'Oh, Mr Hautbois, you must have a corner of my plastic mac,' carolled Miss Colkirk. She had evidently forgiven the unfortunate reference to cucumbers. I didn't much like the look in her eye, but as the alternative seemed to be to eat standing up, I accepted.

'Such a romantic place, isn't it?' she asked the company at large. 'So full of associations! The siege of 1477 - the Duke of Borshire with his six thousand men on top of yonder hill - young John Puttock defying him with a mere twenty-seven faithful yeomen, day and night - the thunder of cannon, the whistling of shot - the, er, cries of the wounded. One feels so involved.'

I'm all for using the imagination, but this, delivered in a mustard-and-ham flavoured voice about six inches to windward of my right lug, was a bit much.

'In actual fact,' I said, 'there wasn't a shot fired. The duke wanted the castle undamaged, so he simply starved them out. The only casualties were three men on the duke's side who died from dysentery. It was all very civilised.'

'But you admit that it's picturesque?' said Dr Bawdeswell.

'Oh, yes. But of course it's far more picturesque as a ruin than it was as a going concern. All you've got now is a few broken walls and that damn great tower, nearly a hundred feet high and only twenty thick. When the great hall and the summer and the winter hall and the chambers and kitchens and butteries were there, with all their roofs and chimneys, it wouldn't have been nearly so dominant.'

'I think I've heard someone say that it's very like some of the smaller Rhine castles,' said Iris. This was true. She'd heard me say it less than an hour before.

'Ah, do you know the Rhine, Miss Overy?' asked Dick Gorlestone. 'I took a party on it last year. Jolly good fun. The lads loved it. Plenty of fresh air and exercise, and some magnificent scenery, of course. We went into a castle there. Can't remember its name, but it had a whacking great tower, rather like this but a bit fatter and shorter. A very fine tower, I thought.'

'Oh, I think this one is *gorgeous*, Mr Gorlestone,' said Iris. 'So deliciously *phallic*, don't you think?'

Definitely an act of provocation. Although it couldn't have been a word that was freely bandied over the Gorlestone tea-table the boy obviously knew what it meant, for he blushed like a stick of rhubarb. Before he or his mother could answer, however, Cyril Thrigby, of all people, took up the challenge.

'Oh, I don't think so,' he said. 'There is a suggestion, perhaps, of -' he hesitated, afraid, perhaps, of shocking us. We held our breath. 'A suggestion,' he went on, 'of the - ah - Alsatian.'

I don't know what I'd expected, but it certainly wasn't a hint of one of the nastier passages of Leviticus. Whether this association occurred to any of the others I don't know, but before any comment could be made he cleared the matter up.

'But in my opinion,' he said, primly, 'for what it's worth, the whole effect is - ah - definitely Germanic rather than Gallic.'

Innocence? Tact? Deafness? Whatever it was, the timing was beautiful. Iris was too clever to attempt a correction; but Dr Bawdeswell was not so subtle. Perhaps he saw himself as the champion of beauty in distress. If so, it was a dreadful misreading of the situation.

'No, *phallic*,' he said. 'Not Gallic. Miss Overy said phallic.'

'Oh, no, Dr Bawdeswell,' said Iris, sweetly. 'Gallic. What was the word you said? Phallic? I don't think I know it. What does it mean?'

He gave an uneasy grin. 'I'm sure you know,' he said.

'No. No, I'm sure I don't. Tell me,' she said, brightly. 'I may find it useful.'

'I'm afraid I must refer you to a dictionary,' he said, rather frigidly.

'Oh, it's one of those, is it? Really, Dr Bawdeswell, I'm surprised you should think that I know a word like that.'

He drooped under her scorn.

'Well, I thought - common knowledge, you know - not an unpleasant word,' he muttered.

Iris turned her back on him.

'I find the air is a little oppressive here,' she murmured, putting an elegant hand to her brow. 'I think I shall go for a little walk, under the trees, where it's cooler.'

'I'll come with you,' I offered.

She ignored me. 'Oh, Mr Gorlestone,' she breathed, leaning towards him and laying the other and equally elegant hand on his arm, 'Would you mind - the heat, you know -'

'Yes, of course,' he said, scrambling to his feet. Together they ambled off to the nearest shady grove. By the time they got there Iris was leaning on him like a consumptive Angelina of the eighteen sixties. He seemed to be standing up well under the strain, stiffened, no doubt, by the thought of Baden-Powell.

Caddow Castle

5

The journey from Caddow to Swynesthorpe Castle is not a long one as the crow flies, but our coach had to keep to the roads, and the bends, banks, and ditches of these, though of deep interest to the historian of the landscape, didn't tempt our driver to put his foot down. In fact, he spent most of the time crouched over the wheel and peering through the windscreen, like Odysseus taking his ship between Scylla and Charybdis. I sat beside him, giving directions and explaining every other minute that I was sorry but this was the only way to get there. Relations rapidly deteriorated, and when he had to negotiate a dog-leg joint in the road by backing into a barley-field he called us a bloody lot of squawking ratbags - a reference, presumably, to the frightened chorus that arose when the bus bumped over a rut or two in the gateway; but it wasn't until we got on to the track that led to the castle and had to make a détour round a faulty cattle grid by way of a field of fine upstanding young beet that he became singularly personal, saying among other things that if I thought his coach was a bloody chieftain tank I ought to have my skull lopped and put in the next bloody exhibition of prize Brazil bloody nuts. There wasn't much, in the circumstances, that I could say. I felt he was quite capable of turning me off and leaving me among the beet. After all, it was his coach.

Swynesthorpe, like Caddow, is a ruin, but at first sight the two places have little else in common. Caddow, dominated by the tower, is built almost entirely of brick, a subtle, accidental mixture of numberless shades of pink, yellow, brown, red, and purple. Swynesthorpe is more stark, more medieval, more, perhaps, of a castle than Caddow. The walls, of flint and fieldstones, are immensely thick, even where the outer skin of clean, black flint has been torn away. At intervals along the wall arrow-slits, and in the later parts, gun-ports, squint across the moat, or rather across the dampish ditch that was once a moat. The walls, though robbed, are still fairly complete in plan, but the only buildings that rise to any great height are the small Elizabethan outer gatehouse and the squat, massive inner gatehouse, which was the first part of the original castle that Sir Henry Swyne, another grand old fifteenth-century bandit, built about 1450. The Swynes had been the sworn foes of the Puttocks of Caddow, except when it suited the two families to get together and stick a combined boot into some third party, and like the Puttocks they had prospered under the early Tudors. By the latter part of the sixteenth century, however, they'd begun to waver a little under the strain of being at the top. Sir Nicholas Swyne, indeed, wavered so much that one day, in the presence of the Virgin Queen, he permitted himself to make a remark that in an unfortunate way expressed a strong doubt as to her right to either title. Only the testimony of several physicians that he was as loopy as a string vest saved him from parting with his head at the hand of the public chopper. He retired to a small circular room in the south-west tower of Swynesthorpe and devoted himself to the pleasures of astrology and in particular to the task of designing a suitable monument for his wife, who had been able to hang on at court through having a certain amount of graft with the earl of Leicester. The simple life suited Sir Nicholas's constitution better than the more sophisticated life of the court suited his wife's, and after her premature death he was able to superintend the construction of the mausoleum. It was a magnificent affair of gilded marble and alabaster, and was decorated with the astrological history of her life. It completely filled the rather small chancel of the parish church, but some of the inscriptions could be read through the windows. There it remained until a Victorian rector, under the influence of the Oxford Movement and a pipe of vintage port, sold it to a contractor, who demolished it and used it as ballast for a small stretch of the new General Metropolitan and East Niffling Railway Company's Line. *Si monumentum requiris, despice.*

It was a good thing Sir Nicholas didn't live to see this desecration; the shock might have killed him. Or again it might not; for after the loss of his wife it was noticeable not only that his health continued to be remarkably robust but also that his interest in monuments and mortality was replaced by an equal passion for muniments and immorality. He descended, both literally and figuratively, from his tower; in Aubrey's felicitous phrase, he left the delights of horoscopy for those of whoroscopy. Moreover, he began to look to his estates, and instructed his bailiffs to recover all the rents, which had fallen into vast arrears during his seclusion. Not that he abandoned astrology altogether; he merely used it scientifically to predict the wealth of his tenants, and adjusted his moveable rents and fines and leases accordingly. As his predictions were invariably optimistic, he prospered. After a dozen happy years, however, some complicated relationship between Aries, the Ram, and Libra, the Scales, gave Sir Nicholas the notion of turning part of the castle into a woollen factory. This was a mistake. The factory itself was a commercial success, but the employment of a large number of young women in such proximity to Sir Nicholas's room proved to be too much of a good thing. Aseries of individual encounters culminated in a prolonged visit to the weaving chamber, and there, surrounded by the ladies of the warp and the woof, he passed away.

His successor, Sir John, was -understandably- a cautious, obscure character, whose only positive act was to choose the wrong side in the Civil War. Parliament sequestered his estate, and the castle had to be demolished and the materials sold to pay off part of the fine. The outer gatehouse, however, was spared, and it continued to be lived in until 1910, when it fell down one Sunday morning while the inhabitants were at church, pointing, no doubt, some sort of moral.

I adorned my tale to the assembled multitude with these and other ornaments, and then took them on a tour of the ruins. While we were inspecting the remains of the privy in the porter's chamber I casually mentioned that it was unfortunately not now in commission, but that if anyone felt the urge there was a modern convenience beyond the eastern wall. There was an immediate thinning of the ranks, but at least I'd said something that genuinely moved them. When we emerged from the gatehouse I saw that the queue stretched from the convenience, an English Heritage unisex one-seater hut, well into the courtyard. As several more of my troop showed signs of disturbance I dismissed them all to do their own thing, with an assurance that I would be on hand if anyone wanted any more information.

By the way the crowd melted away I gathered that they'd had enough for the moment. Iris, I noticed, wandered off with Dick Gorlestone; presumably he did more miles to the gallon than his mother, who was halfway down the queue for the house of easement. Even as I looked the door opened and out came Patty Colkirk. After an initial cast or two she saw me and began to give tongue. I turned hastily away, waved acknowledgement to an imaginary inquirer, and set off for the gatehouse at a steady lope. As I passed through the arch I could still hear her, so I turned to the left and headed for a small, overgrown wood on the north side of the castle, where I reckoned I ought to be safe, for a few minutes at least, from the nattering of the APES. I found a handy log on the dark side of a small glade and sat down to think about Agriculture and the Landscape of Borshire, the subject of my turn that evening.

By and by, when I'd got to the point of wondering what on earth I was going to say that would keep the majority from going straight to sleep, my whorled ear became conscious of the patter of tiny feet. I had just time to slip behind a forked tree before Katherine Southwood trotted into view. She had a faintly hunted look, and I wasn't really surprised when, without seeing me, she went to ground behind a tangle of blackberry bushes. I waited on events with interest. Half a minute later Dr Bawdeswell, perspiration on his brow andsalacity in his eye, broke into the glade. He came to an abrupt halt as I stepped out from behind my tree.

'Ah!' he said, with a twisted smile. 'I don't suppose you've seen - er - anyone?'

'Not a soul.'

He didn't look terribly convinced, but there was little he could do beyond asking me what I was doing. When I indicated, in guarded fashion, that I was about to answer a call of nature, he left.

After a little while the girl stuck her head up.

'I'm afraid they're not quite ripe yet,' I said.

'What?'

'Blackberries. You'll have to wait for the season of mists and mellow fruitfulness. Oddly enough, I was thinking of Keats a few minutes ago. I suppose it was the classical nature of the scene - What men or gods are these? What maidens loath? What mad pursuit? What struggle to escape? What -'

'Lecherous old buzzard!'

'Come, come,' I said, hoping that she was referring to Dr. Bawdeswell. 'A fine scholar, and a pillar of the APES. A bit over the Aristotelian optimum, perhaps -'

'Aristotle's one thing, Slimy Joe's another. Ugh! "Shall I show you the remains of the chapel?", he said -'

'And you fell for that one?'

'I'm nuts on ruins. And there's really supposed to be a bit of a chapel here, though we didn't have time to find it.'

'Let's look together,' I said. 'Or aren't you to be caught twice?'

'Lead on,' she said, picking up a strong piece of wood.

The chapel, when we found it, proved to be a pleasant, melancholy wilderness of flint walls, thorns, brambles, and elder, and we spent a good few minutes poking about and wondering which of the three main lumps of masonry was the putative twelfth-century fragment mentioned by Pevsner.

'I'm glad they haven't got round to clearing it up yet,' she said, hunting down a wild raspberry. 'I like ruins to be ruins, all overgrown and wild and romantic, not something like the Garden of Rest at Borwich Crematorium.'

I agreed, and we chatted of worms and graves and epitaphs for a bit. She seemed to have prowled round most of Borshire's six hundred graveyards, and I warmed to the girl. Her heart, like the rest of her anatomy, was evidently in the right place. At length, rather reluctantly, we thought of moving coachwards. The path was narrow, and she led the way. I followed, admiring her legs in a pure, æsthetic way. They were a pleasure to look at, even - as very few bare legs are - when you got close. Longish, nicely shaped, evenly brown except for a delicious pale region behind the knee, and athletic without being in the least stringy, knotty, or hard. As she was wearing a shortish dress I was able to appraise them at length. I began to feel distinctly friendly, and as our relations seemed to be improving I decided that I ought to make some apology about last night.

'Er - I'm sorry about what happened last night,' I said.

She said nothing. I thought perhaps she hadn't heard, so I repeated it.

She stopped so suddenly that only my quick reflexes, damn them, saved me from bumping into her.

'I don't know how you have the crust to mention last night,' she said, turning fiercely.

I backed into a hawthorn bush.

'Look,' I said, earnestly, 'let me tell you exactly what happened. I know it must have looked a bit odd -'

'Oh, no, quite natural. I wasn't a bit surprised. The first time I saw you I thought "He looks like the sort of man that takes his trousers off in a public corridor".'

'Oh, come now,' I pleaded. 'Be fair. I only took them off because the leg was caught in your door.'

'I also thought to myself "I'll bet he goes in for a spot of night-prowling and I'd better keep my door locked". It's a pity I forgot.'

'Wait!' I cried, partly to stop her train of reasoning, and partly because she was moving off and I was unable to follow. My neck was in the grip of a crutch of hawthorn, and I felt like the clamped-down victim of a Victorian photographer. 'What the deuce has got hold of me?' I demanded, wriggling like hell.

'Hooked at last,' she said, dispassionately surveying my struggles. 'Don't worry, it'll soon be over. A skeleton will add a touch of romance to the place. Black Bill's Thicket, they'll call it. They'll probably put the price of admission up. Or else they'll just think it's a stoat or something that the gamekeeper's strung up. Well, I suppose I'd better help. Hold still.'

She began to fiddle with the branches. Suddenly, with a sharp rending sound, something that felt like a demented gramophone needle ploughed across my shoulders.

'Don't screech, it's only your shirt,' she said. 'You've got another, I suppose? Well, you can always wear a jacket.'

'Thanks a lot,' I said, feeling the wound tenderly. My fingers came back dabbled in gore. 'But to get back to what we were talking about, I must explain that I thought it was my room that you were in.'

'You flatter yourself.'

'I put that badly. What I meant was that I thought your room was mine - oh, hell. Put it this way. The lights were out, so I had to feel my way in the dark, and I miscounted the doors.'

'Oh? How many times?'

'Several,' I said, not wanting to be too specific. 'Yours was the second wrong number.'

'And I suppose you picked up your trophy in the first room?'

'Trophy?' I said, fogged.

'You might call it the Rape of the Belt.'

'Might you?'

'I'll remind you of the plot,' she said, patiently. 'Hercules had to get the belt of the Queen of the Amazons for his ninth labour, and instead of fighting her for it, he - well -'

'Are you suggesting,' I said, 'that I went through all that frightfulness just to nick some woman's belt?'

'As a matter of fact, it wasn't exactly a belt.'

'What, then?'

'You'll see. I left it in your room with the trousers just before we came out this morning.'

'How did you get it, whatever it is?'

'You dropped it in my room.'

'I dropped it? I never touched it. Wait a minute, though,' I said, reflecting. 'I heard a funny sound in the corridor. Like something following me.'

She giggled. 'Did it come when you whistled?'

'I must have got my foot in a loop, or something. Or it got snicked on to my shoe.'

'I suppose it's tactless of me, but who was my predecessor?'

'Well, I came from the direction of the kitchen.'

'The kitchen? Then - oh, gosh, it wasn't - ?'

I nodded. 'It was.'

'She'll love you for that,' she declared, with unseemly relish. 'But you shouldn't have thrown away her gage so soon, and in another lady's room, too. Did she give you that black eye, as well?'

I shuddered. 'Fortunately, she wasn't there. No, I got the shiner from you, or whoever was with you.'

The moment the words were out I realised that they were ill-chosen. She paused for but a moment, then turned and rent me as if I were a mereHimalayan peasant. An impressive performance.

'...and just because you find that one of us doesn't mind sharing her bed, you needn't think we're all like that!' she concluded, breathlessly.

'Who's the one who doesn't mind?' I asked, really more for something to say than for the information.

She stared at me in a nauseated sort of way.

'You're not going to try and tell me that you don't know what I'm talking about?'

'Well, not exactly -'

'I should think not!'

'Look,' I said, trying another bit of coolth, 'what makes you think I've got first-hand knowledge?'

'Oh, nothing much. Just a well-known dressing-gown in your bedroom,' she said. And with that she turned and stalked away.

I followed, not a little disturbed. We moved in an orderly procession over the back moat, through the castle ruins, over the meadow, and through the outer gatehouse to the edge of the car park. There we stopped. There didn't seem to be much else to do, for the car park, apart from half-a-dozen small birds, was empty. The coach had gone.

Swynesthorpe

6

'Damn and blast,' said the girl.

I nodded in agreement. The situation called for enough blasting and damning to supply the whole of Birmingham with good Welsh water. It was now five o'clock, and Great Mardle Hall was distant some twenty-five miles. Supper was at seven, and I was due to begin my lecture at eight. The nearest public road was over a mile away, and although, technically, it was the Queen's highway, I didn't think more than one or two ordinary people, let alone Her Majesty, would be passing along it before sunset. I put these facts to Katherine. She said, coldly, that she knew them already.

'Perhaps Bert can help us,' I suggested, hopefully.

But I couldn't find the custodian. I suspected he'd gone into the woods after a rabbit, thinking, no doubt, that with the departure of the coach he'd seen the last of the bloody public for the day. His bike was still there, and this gave me an idea. Some weeks ago he'd offered to sell me an old machine that was lodged among the lumber at the back of his shed, and I wondered if it were still there. It was. I'd only got a couple of pounds and some odd change, but a brief look at the machine suggested that this was ample, so I left it on his bike with a short note. The contraption I'd bought was an upright model of the early vintage period. It looked as if it might have been put together from parts of a cast-iron bedstead, and the shrunken green leather saddle was cocked more or less vertically in the air. The tyres, though flat, proved to be inflatable, but the front one had an unpleasant carbuncle on it. At the first tentative push on the handlebars the left-hand pedal whipped round and caught me a nasty crack behind the knee. Holding it at arm's length, I wheeled it round to the car park, where the girl was waiting.

'The Old Superb,' I explained, seeing that she was about to ask what I was leaning on. 'Solid Edwardian craftsmanship at its best.'

She observed that there appeared to be no brakes.

'The beauty of this machine,' I explained, 'is that it needs no brakes, being a fixed-wheel job. One simply follows the procedure as laid down in the handbook. On approaching a steep descent, the feet should be pressed hard on the pedals in a direction contrary to that of the motion of the machine, and, to prevent the body rising too violently in the air, the hand should be taken behind the body and should grasp the back of the saddle, thus anchoring the body to the frame. Should one find oneself going down a steep descent backwards, reverse the above procedure. Simple, but effective, and helps to lengthen the arms. Anyway, there aren't all that many steep descents hereabouts, so we should be all right.'

'Did you say "We"?'

'Well, you, then. I can run beside you.'

She said she didn't think she could manage to ride this particular model. She'd ridden some queer objects in her time, but this looked as if it would be akin to cantering along on the spike of a short length of cast-iron railing, and that was an experience she felt she could do without. I must admit I saw what she meant, and sympathised. After all, one had heard strange tales of girls who had had unfortunate experiences during a sharp burst with the Quorn or when *Scuddaway* had two poles down at the rustic, and that must be annoying enough, but it must be even more unsatisfactory to lose one's most precious possession to an Edwardian bicycle.

'All right, then,' I said, getting tough, 'I'll ride it, and you can walk.'

She didn't think much of that, either, and eventually we arrived at a compromise. I would sit on the seat and pedal, while she rode on the crossbar. We used the foundations of the gatehouse as a mounting-block, and after one or two false starts we got going.

It wasn't the most comfortable ride I've ever had. To begin with, the mechanism was infernally stiff, and if there hadn't been a downward slope to the car park I don't think we'd ever have got up enough momentum to keep moving. Then, as the girl was sitting side-saddle on the crossbar, I had to pedal with my knees about a yard apart. The saddle, resembling nothing so much as a scale model of the Matterhorn, gave little or no support, and I had to pull desperately on the handlebars to keep myself pressed against it - a delicate situation, particularly as the track was bumpy. But there were compensations. Two people on a bicycle made for one can't be physically distant. She had one arm round my waist, her shoulder and one nice firm breast were snugged against my chest, and I had her hair in my mouth for most of the time. I couldn't have had a more attractive passenger. On the other hand, she was still a bit disgruntled, and as I hadn't much breath to spare we made little conversation.

We reached the end of the track with no serious damage, but it was certainly a relief to get on to the relatively smooth surface of the road. It was all the more of a shock, therefore, when the carbuncle in the front tyre burst. One moment we were gliding serenely down a slight slope, humming - in my case - the Eton Boating Song, the next - catastrophe: Bang! wibble - wobble - lurch -

fall. The girl and I left the bike together and flew into the ditch. The machine, after doing a fancy pivot on one pedal, followed us.

'Damn and blast!' said the girl, looking down at herself when we stood once more on the road. She'd fallen on top of me, but one hand and one leg had gone into the goo at the bottom of the ditch. She looked as if she were wearing one black glove and half a pair of buskins.

'Never mind,' I said, comfortingly. 'It's good for the skin.'

'Oh, yes?' she said. 'Well, you're going to have the most beautiful bottom in England.'

My trousers, indeed, had received the full treatment. The seat was as soggy as Louisa M. Alcott's masterpiece.

The girl sat down suddenly in the road.

'Are you all right?' I asked. She looked a bit pale.

'Just a little bit mizzly. That damned bike clipped me on the head,' she murmured, and keeled over.

I hauled her to the bank and looked round for ideas. The only house in sight was on the horizon, across about four miles of fields, but on the other side of the ditch was a tall hedge, and a few yards along the ditch was spanned by a rough bridge. On investigation this proved to lead to a small cottage, standing some way back from the road and embowered in gnarled apple-trees. I couldn't see anyone about, so I went back to the girl, half expecting to find that she had recovered. She hadn't, however, and in fact seemed to be rather paler than before. I decided I'd better get her to the cottage, but was dubious about the best way to lift her. Rejecting the fireman's lift, I opted for the Burt Lancaster or parson-at-the-font.

I suppose she weighed something over eight stone, but it felt more like a ton than a hundredweight. I staggered as far as the garden gate, where lo! I found some angel had left a wooden wheelbarrow, up to its ankles in fertile loam. It wasn't in pristine condition. The shafts were a slum tenement for woodworm, and the ravages of time and dry rot had left the bottom looking like a botched attempt at carving a panel of medieval tracery. However, the wheel was almost round, and anyway it was the only form of transport within sight. I lowered the body into it and set off for the cottage. The handles quivered like dowsing rods, but I think everything would have been all right if someone hadn't left a stout rake athwart the path. The wheel struck it with a horrible thud; the front shafts snapped in a little cloud of yellow dust, and the nose ploughed into the path. This forced the handles out of my grasp. The legs did the splits with an élan that would not have disgraced Dame Margot, and the sides and tailboard fell neatly outwards. The girl, still unconscious, lay among the ruins like a dolly-bird topping a do-it-yourself wheelbarrow kit at the Chelsea Flower Show.

I was aghast. I have an almost Forsytian respect for property, even other people's, and what I'd done to the wheelbarrow was deplorable, amounting to trespass or some other proprietary tort. True, the wheelbarrow was still all there, but it was a theoretical, a kind of Platonic, wheelbarrow, and the chances of it becoming functional again were slim. It would have to be replaced, or compensation paid. I stepped to the door and rapped on it. After a couple of minutes of increasing violence I decided that there was nobody at home. The door wasn't locked, however, and a peep inside disclosed a typical late-Victorian interior - deal table, mahogany chairs, stained sideboard, bamboo knockover whatnot, commode, 'Cherry Ripe', 'The Huntsman's Wedding', Queen Victoria, a pair of ebony elephants, a Toby jug, and a fine horsehair sofa. The only inhabitants were an owl and a cat, both stuffed.

The sofa was ideal for my purpose, and no-one, surely, would object to its use for such an humanitarian purpose. I lugged the girl in and laid her out on it. Then I went into the back kitchen to find some water. There wasn't any. No taps, of course, but no water-pail either. There wasn't a drop of liquid in the place. The nearest I came to it was a small phial of almond essence and a few drops of sticky fluid in a bottle labelled 'Clarke's World-Famous Blood Mixture: Beware of Worthless Imitations'. I went back to the girl, rather at a loss. My experience of swooning maidens was, to date, completely literary. Mascall's remedy for swooning in the sixteenth century, I recalled, was to strain or wring the joint of the ring-finger, or to rub it with a piece of gold or saffron. I gave the girl's finger a tweak, but it didn't work. To awaken heavy sleepers Mascall recommended the application of savory boiled in vinegar, but this entailed a little too much preparation, and anyway I wasn't sure that I could lay my hands on either of the ingredients. The same objection applied to the use of a perfume made from old shoe soles or the hoofs of an ass. What the hell did one do for the faints? Unlace the bodice? Rather dubiously I turned the girl on to her side and examined the mechanics. The zip fastener to the dress was the obvious way in, but I hesitated. Supposing someone came in while I was performing my healing arts? What would the girl herself think when she came round and found herself undone? However, after a few seconds' deliberation I decided to risk it. I was already so deep in crime with the destruction of the wheelbarrow that an additional charge of assault or attempted rape wouldn't make much difference. Very gently I unzipped a few inches of her dress and came to the all-important fastening of the bra.

Well, I still don't know how women manage to do the things up behind the back. Admittedly I was a bit unnerved by the sheer beauty of her shoulders, but to my banana-like fingers the hooks and eyes seemed to be riveted together. At last, however, the two ends sprang apart, obviously never to be reunited by the hand of man. Well, that wasn't my concern. But it was a bit disappointing to see no immediate recovery. I rolled her on to her back and waited for the eyes to open, but they remained closed. What now?

Burnt feathers! The classic answer. Guided by Providence, my eye caught that of the stuffed owl. He looked quite benign, as if he might spare a feather or two in a good cause. I turned the glass case around. The wooden back was riddled with worm and was loose at one corner. It was but the work of a moment to insert the blade of my knife and prise open the rotten wood just enough to enable me to slip in two fingers and twitch a couple of feathers from the nearside wing. I found a box of matches on the mantelpiece, and armed with this I went back to the sofa.

No doubt the craft of feather-burning has its own mystery. The species of bird, for instance, may be important, or the age of the feathers. I don't know. But in case the last genuine practitioner of the art is beneath the sod with all his secrets, I'll put it on record that *Tyto alba*, the barn owl, vintage 1890, is a pretty reliable performer. I propped the patient up at the scroll end of the sofa and struck a match. The feathers took a little time to light, but once they'd caught they went away very well, producing a pleasing crackle, a bluish smoke, and a most offensive smell. I waved the brand under the girl's finely chiselled beak, and almost at once she opened her eyes. They were, I noticed, of a fine, clear Vandyke brown.

According to the good old tradition her first words ought to have been 'Where am I?' Instead, she said 'Thank you. I'm sorry to have been such a nuisance.'

'Not at all,' I said, gently. 'It was a pleasure. Welcome back.'

'What's this place?' she asked, staring about her.

I gave her a short *resumé* of recent events, omitting my various remedies. However, her nose was pretty keen.

'What's that terrible pong?' she asked.

'Feathers. The time-honoured method of revival. Burnt under the nose.'

'You caught a hen?'

'Not a hen. Something rather more...'

My voice faded away as we looked at the glass case. Either my tweak had been stronger than necessary, or the owl was a martyr to ringworm. The feathers of the head and facial disc were intact, but all the rest lay in a heap round the bird's feet, leaving the wrinkled skin completely bare. The effect was grotesquely indecent; it was like seeing Mr Gladstone in the nude. I sprang across and covered the case with a handy antimacassar.

'Somebody's coming,' said the girl, who had been giggling irreverently on the sofa.

A heavy tread approached the back of the cottage, and was followed by a scrape of metal as a pail was set down on the tiled floor of the kitchen.

'Anybody at home?' I called out.

A small, bristly man in teashirt, jeans, and rimless glasses came into the room.

'What do you want?' he asked, his voice prickly with suspicion. 'This is private property.'

'Yes, of course,' I said, soothingly. 'But this young lady fell off her bicycle and knocked herself out, and I took the liberty of bringing her in here -'

'Knocked herself out?' he interrupted. 'She looks all right to me.'

'Yes, well, she came round with a bit of help -'

'Do you think I could have a drink of water, please?' asked the girl.

Grudgingly, he went into the kitchen and came back with a glass about a third full. I took it from him and gave it to the girl, who had remained on the sofa.

'This is private property,' he said, resuming his original theme. 'People don't seem to realise that. They come wandering along, and they see a cottage, and they think "ah, yes, what a lovely cottage, let's go in there and have a look and walk about", and they've got no idea of the harm they do. No idea. This is just the most delicate time. Any disturbance could be fatal. Fatal!'

'Fatal?'

'Fatal. My grackles are extremely sensitive.'

'Oh, are they?'

He must have misinterpreted my tone of puzzled enquiry, for he went off like a Roman candle. We gathered that he kept exotic birds, notably Rothschild's Grackles, in cages at the bottom of the garden, and they were always on the point of breeding but were, like so many of us, easily put off their stroke. Our intrusion was just the sort of thing that could gum them up for the season. He ignored our small noises of sympathy and grated on about privacy and property and nosey parkers and philistines who scoffed at him and Darwin and girls who showed all they'd got and sat on valuable chaise-longues when they were covered with mud and expected him to fetch and carry for them when he had his work cut out to keep himself and his grackles going. I was beginning to wonder how on earth we could stop him without being downright rude when Providence stuck another finger in. A denunciatory sweep of his hand touched the antimacassar and it began to slide off the glass case. He pushed it back irritably, and the tide of his rhetoric rolled on for a few more phrases. But then, I suppose, the subconscious surfaced, and he stopped and stared at the antimacassar.

'What's that thing doing?' he demanded.

'Slipping,' I said, bending forward to stop it from revealing all.

I was too late. It slid to the floor.

'Good God!' he said.

We all stared at the owl. It seemed even more obscene than before.

The man turned on me.

'Did you do that?' he shouted.

I did the simple, manly thing.

'No,' I said. Well, we can't all be Washingtons, and strictly speaking I hadn't plucked the thing leaf by leaf.

'I expect it's the moulting season,' said the girl.

For once words seemed to fail him. He just stood there, and his face, normally a kind of greenish-yellow, swelled and reddened like a high-speed nature epic on the Life of a Tomato. Then, with a horrible, grinding scream, he grabbed one of the ebony elephants from the mantelpiece and threw it. Which of us he intended it for must remain a mystery, and perhaps it was as well that there were two of us to disturb his concentration and divide his aim. The thing was well equipped with the usual number of hoofs, trunks, and tusks, and must have weighed all of a couple of pounds. Anyway, neatly bisecting us, it whizzed over the back of the sofa and exploded the glass case containing the cat.

That animal must have been in a delicate, nervous state when it was stuffed, or perhaps it just wasn't used to receiving hostile ebony elephants in the gut. It simply went to pieces. One moment there was this proud black cat, sitting, with a somewhat sardonic look on its face, in front of a saucer of plaster milk; the next there was nothing but a couple of paws and the fag-end of a tail *in situ*, while the rest of *felis domesticus* was distributed about the room. As for sawdust, there seemed to be enough on the furniture and in the air for the next sixteen test matches at Manchester. The little man, however, didn't seem to be alive to the economic possibilities thus opened out.

'Pongo!' he cried in anguish. 'What will mummy say?'

Respecting his grief, we tried to steal silently away. But he saw us, and let out such a cry of rage that we took to flight. The girl led through the door, but I caught her up in a couple of strides and we cleared the ruins of the wheelbarrow together. Down the path to the gate I took a clear lead, and had time to look over my shoulder. The girl was running well but seemed to be holding herself in, with one arm across her body. She was, of course, still undone at the back. I held the gate open for her, and as she passed through we looked back. The little man had been temporarily distracted by the sight of his wheelbarrow, but when he saw us watching him he leapt forward like a gazelle, waving a few fists and calling on us to go there and he'd show us. We set off together down the road at a steady lope. When we reached the corner we looked back again. The little man had given up the pursuit and was wheeling the bicycle into his garden. The spoils of war.

'Perhaps he'll have it mounted and stuffed,' I said, turning to the girl.

She didn't answer, and it struck me that she was regarding me with a certain glint.

'I'm sorry about all this,' I went on. 'I did the best I could.'

'It strikes me,' she said, in a tone that might have come straight from a deep freezer, 'that you had a damn good try to do a little more.'

'I'm terribly sorry about that,' I said. 'It was all I could think of at the time.'

'You don't surprise me in the least. Do you ever think of anything else?'

'I thought it might help you to breathe,' I said, lamely. I must say, even to me it sounded a bit thin, and to the girl it was obviously of less substance than the emperor's new clothes. 'You surely don't think,' I went on, 'that I had any intention of - well - doing anything. After all,' I added, trying to bring a little dignity to the affair, 'I stand *in loco parentis* to you.'

My claim to an honorary place in the Table of Kindred and Affinity didn't seem to reassure her, and I made matters worse by offering to do her up. She said, very huffily, that she thought she could manage without any more help from me, and went behind a tall hedge to prove it. She was gone so long that I began to fear that she'd passed out again, but I daren't look. When she eventually emerged I noticed at once that she'd washed the mud off her leg.

'How's your head?' I asked, hurriedly, hoping to divert her attention from my glance.

'Oh, all right,' she said, coolly.

'If you want any help -' I offered.

'I can manage, thank you.'

And that was about the tone of our conversation for the next two hours. She walked slightly ahead of me until we got to the main road, where we waited in silence until we managed to hitch a lift with a salesman. Unfortunately he confused Great Mardle with East Mardleton, and when we eventually found out the mistake and parted company we were somewhat further from our destination than when we had started. After a couple of miles in the back of a pick-up we transferred to a fast tractor for a spell of cross-country work; then we got a rather tired milk-float, then, for about five miles, a vintage Rolls. Our final carriage was a fish-and-chip van. He was a fine chap, that itinerant vendor. He gave us a plaice and chips each on the house, and went out of his way to set us down at a spot that was less than a mile from Great Mardle Hall. We walked the rest of the way, mostly in silence. I offered a few observations on the beauty of the landscape and the evening, to which the girl assented without any great enthusiasm. In fact, though it really was a most delightful evening it was undeniably chilly, and she was not, of course, overclothed. So we slogged grimly on. As we entered the main gate she said she thought she was getting a blister. This was hardly the conventional olive-branch, but it was the first unsolicited remark she'd made to me since about half-past five, and I thought it might be the first crack in her dudgeon. I was unaccountably anxious to get back on a friendly footing.

'Look,' I said, 'I'm very sorry about that business in the cottage - honestly, I did it in all innocence. I just didn't know what to do to revive you. And I had to do something. After all, you're in my charge, so to speak, and if I'd - well, I hope you won't -'

'Oh, don't worry,' she said. 'I shan't tell anyone. Not even Iris.'

'You can tell who you damn well like!' I retorted, incensed. I marched off, smoking at the ears. After a dozen strides, of course, the generous wrath began to abate and I started to have doubts, not only about my right to be incensed by what was, in the circumstances, fair comment, but also about the blanket permission I'd given her to publish her experiences. I couldn't complain if she told Iris something, at least, of what had happened; but supposing she went to Dr Subcourse, or Mrs Gorlestone? It didn't seem at all likely, but you never know. I'd simply have to trust her. I'd flung the defiance in her teeth, and I couldn't very well attempt to retrieve it. At the worst it would be my word against hers. But my version of the story was certainly not very credible. I marched on, musing.

Just before the end of the drive I glanced over my shoulder. She was some distance behind me, and something in her walk made me turn and hurry back to her. In the woody twilight she looked as pale as a lily.

'Nearly there now,' I said. 'Are you all right?'

'I'm sorry,' she said. 'I feel just a little bit dizzy. I expect it'll pass in a moment.'

'Dop your head between your legs. I'll stop you falling over.' In a few seconds she came up, looking pinker.

'Better?' I asked.

'Much better, thank you.'

We moved off, slowly. It was a peaceful little walk to the end of the drive, and for me, at least, it had a certain dreamlike quality, for my arm, which had supported her while she was bending over, was now about her waist. All too soon we came in sight of the hall.

'Oh, lord!' she said, breaking away.

A Welcome Home Committee was standing in the porch.

Pongo

7

'Two against two, pardner,' I growled, as we drew near the fastest jaws in the Territory. 'This is it. You take Butch Gorlestone, and I'll lay for the Subcourse Kid.'

To leave the allocation of targets until this stage of the proceedings is, of course, inadvisable. Concentration lapses. Moreover, the girl giggled, a thing Wyatt Earp seldom or never did in like circumstances. The result was that we never stood a chance. Dr Subcourse's 'Mr Hautbois!' and the Gorlestones' 'Miss Southwood!' hit us simultaneously, and we stopped dead in our tracks, excuses still firmly in the holster.

And then, stap me vitals! that girl, who by all the rules ought to have been slumping to the deck with a gasp of 'they got me, sheriff', flicked her hair back, walked straight up to them, remarked 'what a lovely evening it is,' and passed into the house, leaving me speechless with admiration.

Not so, however, Butch and the Kid.

'Well, Mr Oh-bwah?' said Mrs Gorlestone.

The reply 'No, not very' rose automatically to the lips, but I suppressed it. The trouble was that I couldn't think of anything else to say, so I just stood there, feeling like a piece of wet string.

'I think, Mr Hautbois, you owe us some explanation,' said Dr Subcourse, clasping his hands in front of him. 'I think you had better tell us where you and that young lady have been.'

Even in this pregnant moment I noticed how his tongue darted out from between his teeth on the breath dental spirant th-, rather like that of a toad I once watched, who was, however, eating bees at the time. I wondered briefly whether to mention this, but decided against it.

'We are waiting, Mr Oh-bwah,' said Mrs Gorlestone.

I kept them waiting a little longer while I toyed with the idea of pretending that I'd been struck dumb. It had its attractions, but it would put my talk on the Borshire landscape seriously in jeopardy, unless, of course, I could undergo a miraculous cure in about twenty minutes' time. On the other hand, there's nothing like telling the truth, and anyway, what had I got to hide? Only the little fact that I'd unhooked Katherine Southwood's bra. A mere slip of the hand. Moreover there was so much else to tell that this part of the story might easily get lost. So I held them with my glittering eye and began at the beginning, which for the present purposes was the viewing of the chapel ruins.

'And where exactly is this chapel?' asked Dr Subcourse.

'Oh, in the very thick of the undergrowth,' I said, hoping to explain our delay in returning to the coach, and at the same time to give the impression that we were intrepid pioneers. 'We had an awful job finding it.'

'It scarcely sounds a suitable place for you to go alone with a young gel,' said Mrs Gorlestone.

'Oh, there was no danger of getting lost,' I explained. 'Anyway, we blazed a trail.'

'I trust you did no damage that might be interpreted as wanton vandalism by our party?' said the doctor.

He would take it like that.

'We must have taken longer over the ruins than I thought,' I went on. 'Anyway, I really think the bus might have waited for us.'

'We held up the departure for at least fifteen minutes,' said Mrs Gorlestone. 'But some of our members were getting impatient for their tea. Moreover, the driver refused to wait any longer.'

'He would,' I murmured.

Then I told them about the bicycle.

'And the custodian was not there, you say, when you took the machine?' asked Dr. Subcourse. 'Will he not think, Mr Hautbois, that some unprincipled person has stolen it?'

I reminded him that I'd left money for it, but he didn't seem to think that £2.53 was an adequate payment. I assured him it was merely a first instalment.

'And was this cycle a lady's machine?' he asked.

For a moment I didn't quite see what he was getting at. Did he think there was some obscure kind of immorality in a man riding a female cycle? He must have seen my incomprehension, for he added:

'I take it that Miss Southwood rode the machine?'

'Oh, I see. No, I sat on the saddle and pedalled, and she rode on the crossbar.'

Mrs Gorlestone uttered a snort of disgust, but Dr Subcourse remained the disinterested, objective inquirer.

'But did this not mean,' he asked, 'that you and Miss Southwood were in - er - extremely close proximity?'

'It was pretty uncomfortable,' I said, dodging. 'But it got us to the road. Then, unfortunately, we fell off.'

'Both of you?' he asked, while Mrs Gorlestone fired off the other nostril.

I explained that, while it's merely difficult for two grown people to ride on a single bicycle, it's well-nigh impossible for them to fall off separately.

'The girl got a knock on the head and fainted,' I added, 'so I had to take her into a cottage just up the road.'

'And how did you get her there if she fainted, Mr. Oh-bwah?'

'Well, I sort of lifted her to the gate, and then I took her up to the door in a crudbarrow.'

'A *crudbarrow?'*

'Wheelbarrow,' I explained. 'A seventeenth-century term. Interesting word, crud. Same root, apparently, as curd. Curds, you know. Goo.'

I'd hoped that this little bit of learning might divert them. It didn't.

'And who was in this cottage that you found so conveniently?' asked the doctor, making it sound as if he thought I'd invented the whole thing.

'Well, at that precise moment, nobody. I had to haul the body by myself and lay it out on the couch.'

'Mr Oh-bwah! Do you mean to say that you carried this young gel into a cottage belonging to a stranger, laid her on a bed, and remained with her, alone?' demanded Mrs Gorlestone.

'Not a bed. A couch - sofa, you know. And I was alone with her only until the owner came.'

'And who was the owner?'

'I didn't get his name, but he breeds Rothschild's grackles. By the way, what exactly are Rothschild's grackles?'

They didn't seem interested in grackles.

'You say Miss Southwood had fainted. What steps did you take to revive her, Mr Oh-bwah?' asked Mrs Gorlestone.

No doubt it'll be marked down against me in the Golden Book that I didn't answer simply and straightforwardly 'well, first of all, I unhooked her bra.' I can't even claim that I tried to say it and failed. I had some vague intuition that they wouldn't understand. So I skipped, figuratively.

'Oh,' I said, 'I burnt a feather under her nose.'

'Mr Oh-bwah! This is no occasion for levity!'

'It's perfectly true. I burnt a feather under her nose, and she came round. As a matter of fact,' I went on, 'I've no need to invent things like that. What actually happened was funny enough.'

I suppose I hoped, as I ran through the catalogue of our misfortunes, that the doctor's lips would twitch and the Gorlestone throat would chuckle, and it would end with the old girl slapping her thigh and declaring that she was damned if it wasn't the funniest thing she'd heard since 'seventy-five, while the doctor would be gasping, as he doubled up for the third time, that it beat all the commercial-traveller-and-farmer's-daughter stories he'd ever heard into a cocked hat. But in fact, as I staggered to the end, the atmosphere, far from being full of camaraderie and back-slapping mirth, was more akin to that of a wet Sunday afternoon in the morgue. My concluding words were followed by a short silence; then Dr Subcourse spoke.

'This is an extraordinary story, Mr Hautbois. Most extraordinary.'

'Yes. But after all, one can see the funny side of it.'

'I fail to see anything humorous in the events you say took place,' said Mrs Gorlestone, heavily. 'In fact I would say that they are verging on the criminal. And then there is the matter of your relations with Miss Southwood. I am not at all satisfied with your explanation of your delay in returning to the charabanc, not at all satisfied. Nor am I satisfied that your account of what happened in the cottage is substantially correct.'

'You are, I believe, a writer of fiction,' put in Dr Subcourse.

'Quite so,' said Mrs Gorlestone. 'I shall question Miss Southwood closely - *most* closely - about the events of this afternoon.'

At that moment a blessed angel of mercy appeared, saving me from the tactical error of calling my temporary employers a pair of crane-gutted slanderous old sods. The blessed angel was Roger.

'Oh, Dr Subcourse,' he said, suavely, 'could I have a word with you about my lecture tonight? I'd like your opinion on a point in the *Preface to Lyrical Ballads*. You see, it's like this...'

They drifted off. Seizing the opportunity, I nipped into the hall and up the stairs, dodging a couple of shots from the Gorlestone. The first thing that caught my eye when I got into my room was a pair of trousers draped tastefully over the bed-rail. I examined them carefully. The seam had come apart, but they weren't a complete write-off. I heaved a sigh of relief and raised my head. Something caught my eye. For a moment life hung fire; then, with one athletic movement, I leapt from the bed, skidded on the slip mat, and shot across the room, taking with me mat, bedside table, water glass, lamp, electric razor, three apples, a banana, and volume I of *Rural Rides*. As I lay there amid the wreckage the Thing leered down at me, a *fin de siècle* combination of steel, whalebone, kid leather, and lace that managed to be both sinister and indecent. I shuddered at the thought of it following me down the corridor the previous night, attached to my leg by one of its malevolant claws. It was, of course, Mrs Gorlestone's corset, hanging at a rakish angle from a nail high up on the wall.

I can't claim that the lecture that evening was one of my more sparkling performances. What with one thing and another I'd had a hard day, and much of what I said seemed to be coming from some sort of internal tape recorder. Moreover, the APES had had a heavy supper, and several of them went to sleep. Not even a long, rambling discourse by Mrs Gorlestone on how her father, the dean, dealt with tenants who persisted in taking two successive crops of wheat, livened things up.

We broke up at half-past nine. I had to spend some time getting my things together, and when I arrived upstairs the kitchen was deserted. I felt distinctly hard-done-by. I'd been sweating my guts out to please them, and as soon as I had time to relax nobody wanted to know me. I made myself a disgruntled cup of tea and withdrew to my tent. There wasn't a great deal of comfort there, either. Iris's dressing-gown and the corset were behind the curtain that served as wardrobe, and together they created something of an atmosphere of apprehension. I hadn't been able to decide what to do with either of them. On the face of it, the dressing-gown was the easier problem, but I wasn't at all sure how I stood with Iris, as I hadn't really spoken to her all day.

I began, wearily, to mop up the water that I'd spilt before the lecture, and I'd just about got everything back to normal when there came a soft knock at the door. It was Iris.

'Hallo, William,' she said, and her voice started my back hair pricking. 'May I come in?'

'Yes, of course. Excuse the mess.'

As a matter of fact, apart from the bedside lamp glowing away on the floor, there wasn't any mess, but one says these things.

She came in and sat down on the edge of the bed. I took the basket chair.

'I had to drink my tea in solitary stir,' I said, making conversation. 'The place seems deserted. Where is everyone?'

'Oh, here and there. In the common-room. Bed. A few of us went for a stroll in the park, down by the lake.'

'The idle rich. Anyone interesting?'

'Roger Barton-Bendish was there with Sandra. Dr Bawdeswell - Mrs Setch - Mr Thrigby - Dick Gorlestone - Katherine with her Tony.'

'The heart-throb of the campus.'

'Well, you can't complain, William dear. You managed to get her all to yourself at Swynesthorpe. Tony wasn't at all pleased about *that.'*

'A mere accident,' I said. 'We missed the coach simply because we got interested in the ruins of the chapel.'

She laughed. 'You don't expect me to believe that, do you?'

'It happens to be the truth.'

'Oh, William dear, don't get horrible and stuffy. God knows, I've had enough of that all day. I only meant you might have thought up a better story. I expect you went to the chapel, but you must have been there a good half-hour.'

'No, nothing like that. We went to look at the ruins, because she said she'd like to see them, and I went with her. We just happen to be interested in ruins, both of us.'

'Is that really all there was to it?'

'Yes.'

'You just talked about Decorated tracery and Early English arches, I suppose?'

I nodded.

'How sweet,' she said, thoughtfully. 'And how characteristic.'

I sensed some hidden criticism here. Could she be thinking of my failure to return to her last night? Some explanation of that would be in order, and might shift her attention from Swynesthorpe.

'To change the subject,' I said, 'I'm really very sorry about last night.'

'Oh?' she said, coldly. 'Which part do you regret most?'

'Let me tell you exactly what happened.'

'Is that necessary? I expect when you got downstairs you found you'd rather go and look at the ruins of an old garden shed.'

'Oh, pipe down and listen,' I said, irritably. I'd had, remember, a hard day.

Rather to my surprise she piped down, and heard in silence an abbreviated version of my experiences last night after I'd left her bedroom.

'So that's why I didn't return your dressing-gown last night,' I concluded. 'I ought to have brought it back tonight, but I wasn't sure how you'd receive me.'

'But, you poor lamb,' she said, reproachfully, 'did you think I was angry with you?'

'Well, you seem to have been avoiding me all day.'

'But, darling, I mustn't be with you all the time. You know what gossips these old ladies are. Darling, I've a little headache - could you turn the main light off?'

I did so, leaving the bedside lamp shining bravely on the floor.

'People talk so,' she went on. 'They'd say the most dreadful things about us if we gave them the chance. I ought not to be here, you know. Think what Mrs Gorlestone would say if she knew I was sitting on your bed! I really ought to sneak back to my room.'

'No, don't go yet,' I said, meaning it. She was neatly attired in a short green skirt and a close-fitting, sleeveless blouse. 'You look extremely ornamental.

The sort of thing no bedroom should be without.'

She smiled. 'William, darling, you mustn't say things like that at this time of night. I'm too impressionable. I really must go. Could I have my dressing-gown, please?'

'Well, if you must,' I said, sighing. 'It's behind the arras.'

'I hope it's not too muddy,' she said, getting up. 'I expect it'll brush off. In here, did you say?'

She reached for the curtain, but I was there before her, having, by some sort of athletic miracle, whizzed out of the chair and over the corner of the bed.

'I'll get it!' I gasped.

'William, dear!' she said, looking at me with enormous, startled eyes. 'I believe you've got a guilty secret.'

'No, no,' I said, hastily. I had, of course. The corset.

'Oh, but you must have. I think you've got another woman in there.'

'No, no. It's just that - well, I don't think you should see the, er, clothes in there. They're a little - well, I mean - they're not really fit -'

'Oh, darling!' she gurgled. 'How intriguing! You make them sound positively indecent. I *must* see them.'

She sidestepped and grabbed at the curtain. I sidestepped too, and caught her by the wrist. She began to struggle. I put my other arm around her back.

'Do you tango?' I asked, politely.

She laughed, and made another effort to get at the curtain. We swayed, did a fancy step or two, blundered over the basket chair, and, still loosely entangled, collapsed on to the bed. She lay so still for a moment that I thought she'd hurt herself; then she raised her face, parted her lips, and closed her eyes.

'Darling,' she said, a minute or so later, 'let's get comfortable, shall we? And take your shoes off. I don't want to get laddered.'

I took my shoes off as she moved further up the bed. Somehow or other her skirt had become bunched about her hips, revealing a pair of exceptionally well-shaped thighs, and as she lay back on the pillow her blouse, operating on some inbuilt destruct mechanism, burst open. The effect was disturbing. In fact, it was so like a sexual fantasy that for a few moments I wondered whether my hard day was not bringing on an hallucination. I put my hand out and touched the nearest part of her anatomy, which happened to be a knee. It seemed real, and the thigh above it was beautifully firm.

'Darling!' she murmured.

I lay down and took her into my arms. We began to kiss. Presently I slipped my hand through the gap between blouse and skirt. As I stroked her smooth, warm back she pressed herself against me and started to writhe, giving me a curiously buoyant, nautical feeling.

'Darling,' she whispered, 'you can undo me if you like.'

Ruskin, in his rubric to Holman Hunt's picture 'Awakening Conscience', interprets thus: 'The poor girl has been sitting singing with her seducer; some chance words of the song, "Oft in the stilly night", have struck upon the numbed places of her heart; she has started up in agony; he, not seeing her face, goes on singing, striking the keys carelessly with his gloved hand'. Putting aside for the moment the question of Victorian seducers playing the piano in gloves, the point I'd like to make is that in one respect at least there was a distinct analogy between my situation and that of the lady in the picture: we were both put off our stroke by a reminder of past times. In her case, the agent was some phrase of the poet Moore; in mine, a pair of hooks and eyes. The touch of my fingers on the fastening of her bra was enough to conjure up the scene in the cottage at Swynesthorpe. We were no longer alone together in the room; we had an owl, a cat, and an insensible girl on a horsehair sofa for company.

It's a moot point whether in such circumstances a loss of concentration is in itself a sufficient reason to attempt disengagement. A purist, no doubt, would have unclinched immediately, but I wasn't a purist. And I was vaguely sure that it wasn't just a simple lack of concentration that was putting the mockers on me. Perhaps there was a feeling that I was well on the way to doing what the Southwood girl thought I'd done last night, and, subconsciously, I didn't want to lose that little bonus of righteousness that one gets when one is undeservedly accused. Perhaps the events at Swynesthorpe had made a bigger impression on me than I'd realised. Anyhow, whatever it was, I suddenly felt that, much as I liked Iris, I couldn't at that moment proceed to the right true end of love. I began to wonder how I was going to break the news to her.

For it's one thing to decide that you want to call it a day, and quite another to tell this to a red-hot girl who has just put her hand inside your shirt and seems intent on carving her initials on your chest. A straightforward explanation simply wasn't possible, and a plea of fatigue, however genuine, would have been tactless. I didn't want to say anything that would hurt her. And even as I wondered what to do the situation became more critical. I'd been absent-mindedly fiddling with the latchings of her bra, with no intention of undoing them; but they were either faulty or a different pattern from the girl Southwood's, for now, reacting to a quick twitch of her shoulders, the hooks and eyes parted company, and the whole thing fell away.

If I was going to stop this was surely the last possible point. And if I wasn't to appear crude and callous the only way was to create a diversion. I raised my head slightly and looked round for help, while continuing to knead and stroke.

My eye fell on my electric shaver. When I'd cleaned up I'd left it lying, plugged in, on the bedside table. It was normally a quiet machine, but the bang it had received when I knocked it off the table had altered its gentle, gnat-like hum to a rather savage whirr. It would, at least, provide an interruption. I raised myself slightly to reach it. The movement, which brought our lower halves into extremely close contact, evidently left her in no doubt of the effect she was having on me.

'William, darling!' she breathed, and her hand began to move downwards.

It was now or never. I pressed the switch. There was an instant, splenetic buzz.

'Hell's bells!' I cried, with a flash of inspiration. 'A hornet!'

I leapt off the bed, and seized the only weapon to hand, a shoe. My first swipe caught the lamp a fearful crack and it went out. I dropped on my hands and knees and, while beating the carpet with one hand, searched for the flex of the shaver with the other. After some agonising moments I found it.

'Got it!' I said, jerking the plug out and shoving the whole contraption under the bed. 'Are you all right?'

'Yes, thank you. Are you sure it's dead?'

'As mutton. Shall I put the light on?' I asked, moving towards the main switch.

'Oh, no, William darling. Not yet.'

I felt my way to the bed and sat down. My diversion had been only partially successful. I stood up and squared my chest, prepared to make a manly statement. But before I could utter there was a tap at the door.

'I say, Bill old chap,' said Roger, opening the door a crack. 'Are you asleep?'

I sprang across the room. The deepest of snores wouldn't keep him from trying to wake me, so the immediate problem was to stop him coming in.

'Just a minute,' I said. 'Had an accident with the light. Broken glass. Probably a live wire too. Stay there. Be with you in a minute.'

I shut the door and went back to bed.

'Iris,' I whispered, 'get behind the wardrobe curtain. Wrap yourself in the coverlet if you like. I'll try to keep him out of the room, but you'd better hide, just in case.'

I waited till the rustles had died down, then sneaked across to the door and opened it a crack.

'Something terrible's happened,' said Roger. 'I say, can I come in?'

'Well -'

'I don't want to broadcast it over the whole house, and I need your help, Bill old man. I'm in the deuce of a hole.'

'I told you she was too young.'

'No, not that,' he said, pushing the door. 'You're not very hospitable tonight. Have you got a woman in there?'

'Just a live wire.'

'Ah, hell, who cares? I'm shockproof now,' he muttered, getting a foot through. To avoid an undignified scene I let him in, hoping that Iris was well concealed. He sat down on the bed. I left the door slightly ajar, so that a little of the corridor light came through.

'Well,' I said, 'what's the trouble?'

'Have you studied my programme closely?'

'Well, what with one thing and another...'

'The high spot of the week was to be tomorrow evening's lecture. Or rather, recital. Selections from the poems of William Wordsworth, to be read by Morley Swanton.'

'The Morley Swanton?'

'Who else? The critic, poet, novelist, broadcaster, etc. I met him at a party in London, and he said he'd come.'

'At a party? Wasn't that a bit risky?'

'Well, yes, as it turned out. I sent him a letter reminding him last week, but as I didn't get any answer I thought I'd better give him a tinkle tonight. And do you know what he said?'

'He'd been called to the bedside of a sick aunt?'

'No, no, old boy. I don't suppose he's got any aunts. He's about a hundred and ten himself. No, he said he couldn't remember anything about it, and he wouldn't come to a God-forsaken hole like Mardle for anything under two hundred quid. And anyway he's speaking to the Tennyson Society tomorrow night. Rot him!'

'Put not your trust in princes,' I said, soothingly. 'Well, so what? You're simply one dodderer short. Can't you give them a few rousing numbers from the Works yourself? I'm sure they dote on you. They'll lap it up.'

'Oh, the audience is all right. I'm not worried about them. It's old Subcourse that's the snag. I've been building up old Morley Swanton as the high spot, famous doyen of Wordsworthian scholars, poet of distinction, and all that codswallop, and how bloody clever I was to get him for this course, all with a view to boosting my chances of getting the Resident Officer job. And what's the old puff adder going to say when I tell him that the great Swanton isn't coming? He'll ask why. And when I have to confess that I made a great balls-up of the whole thing, my chance of the job will be floating down the river with the rest of the flotsam.'

'Roger,' I said, 'my heart bleeds for you. But I don't see what I can do. I don't know any critics or poets of distinction. I suppose,' I added, laughing lightly, 'that you want me to assume some sort of imbecilic disguise and pretend to be Morley Swanton?'

'Dear old lad!' said Roger. 'You took the words out of my mouth.'

'Oh, no!' I said, aghast.

'Bill, old friend,' said Roger, wheedling like mad. 'You know how much this job means to me?'

'What about me?'

'Look, be reasonable,' said Roger, shifting gear. 'You must admit that your chance of landing it is about one in fifty thousand after this afternoon. You should have heard old Subcourse muttering about you at the supper-table. He'd rather have something drawn by lot out of the ape-house than you. Oh, I realise that it wasn't your fault, but you know what Herr Director is. Once damned, always damned. And anyway, we'll manage so that he won't know it's you.'

'Oh, yeah? How do you propose to do that? Pinch his glasses?'

'Nothing so elaborate. No, we simply dress you up as Wordsworth.'

'No!'

'Bill, old man,' said Roger, 'I thought you were a friend. I can't believe you wouldn't do this little thing for me. Look me in the eye - why in hell's name,' he demanded, 'are we sitting in the dark? How can you look me in the eye when there isn't a fluid ounce of light in the room?'

And before I could stop him he got up and switched on the main light.

I shot a quick glance at the curtain. It was closed, and the folds hung demure and innocent. But they didn't hang far enough. They stopped short of the floor by about fifteen inches, and it didn't need the eye of an eagle to see two size five feet in tights standing there. I stood up.

'All right,' I said, ushering Roger to the door. 'I agree in principle. But I don't see how in the world you expect to pull it off. I mean, won't Dr. Subcourse know Morley Swanton?'

'No, he's never met him. Old Swanton's a bit of a hermit. It was only by chance that I met him, when he came out of hibernation to visit a friend of mine. That was why it was such a coup to get him. And if you're wondering about the period clobber, don't worry.' He held up a key. 'This'll let us into the costume room, and I happen to know they've got a complete set of Regency gear there.'

'Yes, but what about my face? They'll spot who I am in the first two seconds.'

'Simple. There's a splendid piece of fuzz there, just waiting to spring to your noble jaw. It'll cover all the natural defects.'

'But Wordsworth hadn't got a beard.'

'A detail,' said Roger. 'Who the hell's going to worry about that? Come on, laddie, let's go and kit you out. No time like the present. What a pal! And what a fantastic organiser I am! Nothing forgotten.'

When I got back Iris had gone.

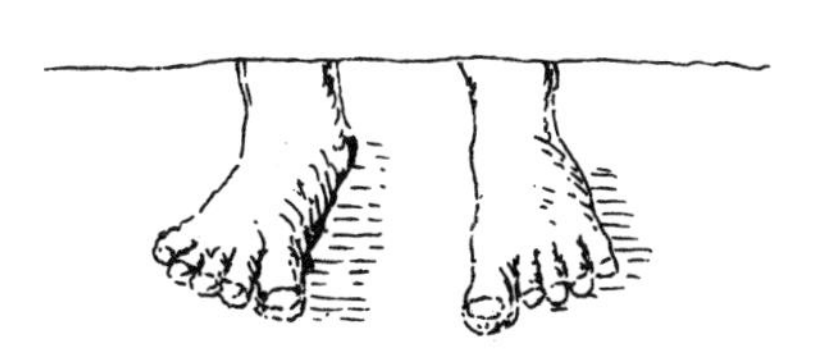

A pair of size 5 feet

8

The morning dawned bright and fair. At least it was bright and fair by the time I woke, which wasn't exactly at dawn. My spirits didn't quite match the weather, for the thought of the foul deed I'd promised to do for Roger was strong within me. When I got down to the dining-hall the old stomach did a roll-and-bucket at the smell of the first fried egg, and one glance at the assembled APES getting theirs brought all my latent misanthropy to the surface. I looked round for a decent, isolated, lonely table, preferably with only one chair and that facing into a corner. Unfortunately the hall was pretty full, and I spied Miss Patty Colkirk moving towards me with a predatory gleam in her eye; so I flopped into the nearest vacant chair, and applied myself to the Honey Popsies as if I were breaking a ten-day fast. It wasn't until I was crunching the third mouthful that I looked up and realised that I was sitting opposite Miss Honey Popsie in person, Katherine Southwood. Less pleasing was the realisation that next to her was Tony Saham. Today the shirt was plum-coloured and the cord jacket a silky fawn. He was delivering the fag-end of a mini-lecture on Jacobinism in Borwich during the Napoleonic Wars, and it wasn't until my plate was empty that he paused.

'Hello,' I said, having crunched the last mouthful. 'Jolly good stuff, this. Rothschild's Grackles, I believe.'

Katherine giggled.

'What's the joke?' asked Saham, his glance flecked with suspicion.

'Oh, nothing much;' I said. At least she hadn't told him about it.

'Come on, share it with us.'

'I suppose it wasn't really very funny,' said Katherine.

'One of those esoteric jokes, I'm afraid,' I said, pouring oil on the flames. 'I don't think a third party would get much out of it.'

'Try me,' he said, leaning forward and planting both elbows on the table. The left one, I noted with satisfaction, landed on a large blob of marmalade.

'Well, it was like this,' I began. Then a what-the-hell socked me in the gizzard. 'On second thoughts, no. It's hardly a fit story for mixed company at the breakfast table.'

'What the hell do you mean?' he demanded, leaning further forward.

'Really, young man,' said my neighbour, Miss Catton, drawing in her chin and fixing him with a bright, bird-like eye. 'Your manners are abominable.

Please behave yourself. And you have marmalade on your arm.'

'Oh, my God,' said Saham. He gave his sleeve a perfunctory glance, got up, and stalked out.

'Now,' said Miss Catton, with a coy smile, 'you two young people can have your little chat.'

That, of course, turned us to stone, and for a few moments I thought the rest of the assembly had heard the remark and were waiting, breathless, on events, for the noise of champing teeth and idle chatter died suddenly away; but it was only Dr Subcourse manifesting himself, preparatory to his ceremonial announcements. After the technical details of time, place, and personnel, however, he folded his hands in front of him and bowed his head, like a guard of honour at some lying-in-state. I had a fleeting feeling that he was going to announce that someone had passed away in the night.

'Ladies and gentlemen,' he said, after a lengthy pause that had one or two people shifting uneasily. He raised his head, and fixed a grave, calculating eye on the portrait of Winifred, Lady Mardle, which hung at the far end of the hall over the dirty plates trolley, 'I have a rather unpleasant duty to perform. The night before last - Sunday night, that is - the bedroom of your president-elect, Mrs Gorlestone, was broken into. A certain amount of damage was caused, and an article of clothing - I shall not, of course, be more specific - was abstracted. Mrs Gorlestone immediately informed me of the offence, and we took counsel together in order to formulate a course of action. We could, of course, have called the constabulary, but we felt that such action might be rather precipitate in view of the possibility that the offence had been more in the nature of a thoughtless prank than a deliberate theft. The offender has now had twenty-four hours in which to return the garment. I regret to say that he - or she - has not seen fit to do so. We are, however, determined to be as lenient as possible in the circumstances, and so we have agreed to allow another twenty-four hours' grace. If the article has not been returned by that time, however, with a full apology for its abstraction, we shall have no alternative but to take further action. I might add that we have the strongest suspicions of the identity of the culprits, but we feel that we must give them a last chance to own up to this stupid prank. Thank you.'

So, I thought, tonight looks like being a busy time. Not only do I have to wade through acres of lush, ankle-high Wordsworth looking, and probably sounding, like the patriarch Abraham, but also I have to work out some way of getting the corset back to Mrs G. without being discovered. What a life! By the end of the week I'll certainly have earned my miserable fee.

The day was dedicated to a study of the flora and fauna of Borshire, with an illustrated lecture followed by a coach excursion. Our lecturer and guide was Carleton Forehoe, the county's most eminent, or at least most publicised, naturalist. He was a small, rufous man with a high, grating voice, and from the back of the room, where I'd retired after making the introduction, much of the lecture sounded like a couple of cock pheasants in the mating season. The audience loved it, although I suspected that a few of the older, deaf-aided members thought he was actually doing bird impressions. During question-time one old girl asked him if he'd ever thought of going on the radio like Percy Edwards, which was a nasty one for a man who had his own five-minute spot on television every Thursday tea-time.

After the lecture we coffeed and encoached. There was the usual jockeying for places, and by the time I got in I found that the only vacant seat in the vehicle was being kept warm for me by Patty Colkirk's vast mitt. I bowed to the inevitable and resolved to keep a stiff upper lip. This, in fact, fitted in very well with Miss Colkirk's style of conversation, which relied heavily on the rhetorical question; but I wasn't sorry when we drew up at our first debussing point. This was West Niffling Heath, blasted by the army until a year or two before and now handed over to the Borshire Naturalists' Association as a nature reserve. I'd carefully avoided mentioning the earlier history of the area to any of the party, for although the army had delivered it with a clean bill of health there was always the possibility that the disposal experts had missed the odd mortar-bomb or anti-tank shell, and I didn't want to pass up the chance, however statistically remote, of seeing Mrs Gorlestone rise from the ground like feathered Mercury and drop as the gentle rain from heaven. The likelihood was, however, that one clump from a Gorlestone hoof would convince any sensible mortar-bomb that you can't win 'em all, so I wasn't very sanguine. I'd kept quiet about the grisly past, but Mr. Forehoe wasn't so delicate. The first thing he said when he'd got us together a hundred yards from the coach was 'Well, this used to be an artillery range not so long ago. The soldiers tell us they've cleared it, but we've come across a few odd things. We keep them in the glory-hole over there' - he gestured towards a derelict hut a few yards away - 'I shouldn't go too near it if I were you. These things tend to get a little unstable, I'm told, especially in warm weather. Don't want any little accidents, do we?'

This tactful approach to the subject sent half-a-dozen of our less intrepid members back immediately to the coach, at least two of them muttering that the wind was too cold for them. It was, in fact, a singularly windless day, and the temperature in the shade, if there'd been any shade, would probably have been in the eighties. The rest of us, realising that in half-an-hour the motionless coach would be a hell-hole unfit for man or beast, grabbed our lunch packets, girded up our loins, and followed Mr Forehoe, who was already powering his way through gorse and heather. I took up my station at the rear, foreseeing that my job would be to help lame dogs over stiles.

And so it proved. Not stiles exactly, but barbed wire, bogs, and abandoned trenches. By the time I'd got our anchor-man, Mrs Attlebridge, through the first fence the rest had disappeared, but we put in a spurt and, topping a small rise, saw the rest of the company strung out over a vast plain, and moving with the slow, dogged gait that one always associates with the tribal migrations of prehistory. Even at that pace they drew away, and we only caught up when they halted to bivouac in a small dell overlooking Great Nifflemere, a fine stretch of open water created in 1845 by the third Earl of Niffle with the help of unwilling hands from the local union workhouse. The elders of the tribe, sweating after their long trek, had stripped off, and the first impression one got was of a revolting acreage of bare flesh.

Wolfing a lukewarm sardine sandwich, I sat down. Iris, in a simple but sophisticated silk blouse and shorts, was a few yards away, sitting in a group of attendant satyrs - Cyril Thrigby in pin-stripe, Dr Bawdeswell in a niggly check, and Dick Gorlestone in flannels and a blazer. The whole group looked less like *Déjeuner sur l'herbe* than an unsuccessful *montage* advertising the New, Fantabulous Creamy Flavour of Crummies, the Bar with the Heart of Gold. The girl Southwood, on the other hand, blended so well that it was some minutes before my roving eye picked her up. It's true she was further away than Iris, but she was definitely part of the prospect that pleases. Her companion, however, fulfilled Bishop Heber's immortal antithesis. What the hell was Saham doing on Historic Borshire? I decided to investigate.

'Giving the Romantics a miss?' I asked.

He turned a languid eye up at me. 'Only Barton-Bendish on Coleridge, and I've already heard that lecture twice. There was nothing on this afternoon. All right to come on your outing? Kay said you wouldn't mind.'

'No, of course not. I hope you'll find it interesting.'

'It's a nice day, anyway. Ah!' he said, lying back in the grass.

I glanced at Katherine. She was staring abstractedly into the distance, as if she were in the middle of a meditation on Saxon apsidal churches. She had her hands clasped about her knees, and her tactile values were irresistible. It seemed the most natural and desirable thing in the world to lay my hand on her shining hair. The actual touch, of course, brought me up sharply, and I whipped the paw back in. Not before Saham had noticed it, however.

'Cramp,' I explained, waggling it freely. 'Lack of salt.'

Saham grunted, and the girl made a noise that could have been either a suppressed laugh or an expression of tight-lipped scorn. I sat beside and slightly behind her, and looked at her hair. Then I caught Saham's eye on me, and hastily transferred my gaze to a clump of scots pines about three miles past her right ear. Saham didn't intimidate me, but he undoubtedly had first claim on her.

We sat in silence for a minute or two. Then Saham scrambled to his feet.

'It's too hot here,' he said. 'What about a stroll down to the mere?'

From his confidential tone I guessed that he didn't intend me to be one of the party, but I got up all the same.

'Yes, it's cooler down there,' I said.

He glared briefly at me.

'I'm comfortable here,' said Katherine. 'You two can go.'

'Oh, come on, Kay,' he said, appalled at the prospect. I can't say I was too thrilled about it, either.

'No, I'll stay here. You go and cool off.'

'I'm not too hot,' he said.

'I thought you said you were.'

'What a fine view this is,' I said. 'I think I'll stay put.'

Saham groaned and flung himself down. Only this time he was between me and Katherine. I sidled round behind them and sat down next to her. He snorted.

'Bless you,' she said.

We had another trappist session, lasting this time three or four minutes. Saham was the first to break.

'Are we staying here all day?' he demanded.

'Oh, no,' I said, playing it straight back to him.

The next one came out of the back of his hand. 'I suppose this is one of your days off?'

'More or less.'

'Hadn't you better start rounding them up?' he asked, trying to get me to lash out.

'I'll give them a few more minutes.'

'Didn't I hear someone calling you?' he said, after a short pause.

'No,' I said. 'It was a pheasant.'

'Game to Mr Hautbois,' said the girl. Wrong sport, of course. 'Here comes one of your girl-friends, Mr Hautbois,' she added.

'Oh, hell,' I said, staring straight ahead. 'Not the Colkirk woman?'

'Oh, I didn't know about her,' she said, sweetly. 'No, it's Iris.'

'Come on,' said Saham, getting up again. Restless type. 'Let's go for that stroll now, Kay.'

I got up too, feeling that the Great Playwright was getting a little repetitive in his old age.

'Oh, Katherine, dear,' called Iris, from a few feet below us.

We waited for her to come up to us. She wasn't exactly panting, but her bosom was heaving in a way that was very attractive, and a small insect clinging to the lower slopes was looking undeniably green about the gills.

'What a delicious day,' she said, sitting down and fanning herself with a sheet of Mr Forehoe's nature notes. 'Katherine, dear, I've been wanting to see you all morning. Ah, Tony. Dr Bawdeswell would like to have a word with you about one of your cultural influences. He's discovered some absolutely marvellous fact about John Bunwell. I think his grandfather was born in 1701 instead of 1703, or some frantically interesting titbit. Anyway, I promised to send you over to him. And William, dear, Mrs Gorlestone wants *you*. Urgently.'

'I think you want to get rid of us,' I said.

'Actually,' said the girl Southwood, who was still seated, 'Tony and Mr Hautbois are just going down to the mere. I think Tony's got something interesting to tell Mr Hautbois, haven't you, Tony? Go on, off you go, together.'

I have no doubt that Saham would have preferred Dr Bawdeswell's nonsense to my company, just as I would have preferred Mrs Gorlestone's bloody-mindedness to his; but at the girl's bidding we turned and trudged down the slope like a pair of zombies. We didn't say much as we walked. As a matter of fact, we didn't say anything until we came to the edge of the mere. Then I remarked that it was cooler down there. He grunted. As he seemed to have something against the temperature as a topic of conversation, I switched to academic subjects.

'And how,' I asked, using the gambit recommended in the Useful Phrases appendix to the University Handbook, 'is the research?'

'Oh, I'm just about to begin a new - do you really want to know?'

'No.'

We contemplated the water of the mere for a couple of minutes in silence. I couldn't think of anything to say - at least, that would draw a civil response. What I wanted to ask was 'What the hell does Katherine Southwood see in a nitpicking pratt like you?' but I doubt if he would have answered in temperate fashion. Eventually I remembered something the girl had said.

'And what,' I asked, still courteous, 'was it that you wanted to tell me?'

He swung round to face me. 'You know damn well what.'

'Do I?'

'Yes.'

'Something about John Bunwell?' I asked, groping.

'No.'

'Caddow? Swynesthorpe?'

'No!'

'Borshire agriculture?'

'NO!'

'I give up. Tell me.'

He took a step towards me. 'Kaismigal!'

'What?' I said, baffled. 'Kaismigal?' It had a vaguely Himalayan ring about it.

'Kay's - my - girl,' he said, spitting it out in pieces.

'Strewth,' I said. I'd never thought to hear any flesh-and-blood individual actually mouth the old cliché. Definitely one for the log.

'Look, I'm telling you, keep away from her,' he went on. 'You've been hanging about her right from the first. Well, we're fed up with having you breathe down our necks.'

'I don't remember breathing down *your* neck yesterday,' I said.

'Don't try to be funny. Look, never mind what happened yesterday. I'm telling you to leave her alone now. I suppose you think that just because you're the damned tutor you can have any woman you like. Well, you can't have this one. Anyway, she hates your guts.'

'Well, she doesn't seem to mind the rest of me.'

For a moment I thought we were going to indulge in a bout of fisticuffs. The rest of the company would have had a grandstand view of the contest, and perhaps it was this that decided him against attempting to tap the claret.

'Look, Hautbois,' he said. 'I'm telling you. Stay away from her, that's all. Do you get that?'

'No. I'm thick. Are you trying to tell me something?'

He turned away and strode up the hill. As circumstances had it, I didn't have a chance to get near Katherine, for by the time we got back the APES were folding their tents and preparing to resume the trek, and I was forced back to my role of sheepdog and straggle-master. Mr Forehoe set his usual sharp pace, and in a few minutes he was out of sight of the rearguard, which consisted of myself, Mrs Attlebridge, and Patty Colkirk. The next hour was pretty hellish, what with Miss Colkirk's Peter-pannery and Mrs Attlebridge's unfortunate tendency to get bogged down and wired up. However, we ploughed on, picking up a fallen woman here and there, and missing, of course, all Mr Forehoe's words of wisdom on the greater snotweed and the red-winged dodman. These must, in fact, have been delivered to a gradually decreasing band of enthusiasts, for a rough count at the top of a rise showed that the lame, the halt, and the blind around me numbered two-thirds of the entire party. Also revealed was the coach, a couple of hundred miles away on the horizon, and a motion to make a beeline for it was carried with acclamation. An hour later we clambered aboard, beating the official party by a couple of rumps. By the time everyone was seated it was three o'clock. This meant that our visit to the Slurrupham bird sanctuary had to be cut to a bare half-hour, for we were booked for tea at the Slurrup Arms at four o'clock, and tea was the one thing that couldn't be skipped or rushed. In fact, when the time came tea seemed interminable, mainly because I was stuck at a table with Patty Colkirk, Mrs. Attlebridge, and Cyril Thrigby. And the coach journey back was pretty lousy, too, for I drew Miss Colkirk again. And when I wasn't listening to her chatter, I was thinking about the experience, almost certain to be traumatic, that I was to go through that evening.

You'd have thought that, what with one thing and another, Fate would have considered that it had already done an honest day's work on me, and would have had nothing more in mind for itself than a quiet evening, with pipe and glass in hand, slumped in a comfortable chair before the celestial telly. But no. The porter met me in the hall of Great Mardle with the news that there was a message for me in the secretary's office. He said sooth. It was a note from Peter Wood-Norton, and it read:

'Awfully sorry but can't oblige you tomorrow, as have had urgent call to go and see aunt Emmy who has plague in Bognor and you know who aunt Emmy is the one with the goodies stuffed away in Barclays. So sorry. All I can do is to leave you notes and a few odd books if you want to give them anything. Also a box of pot. The rest of the day should be alright as C. Tittles-Hall will show you round and his lordship is on the ball with his barrows. So sorry. Yours Peter.'

So the sick aunt had really come home to roost.

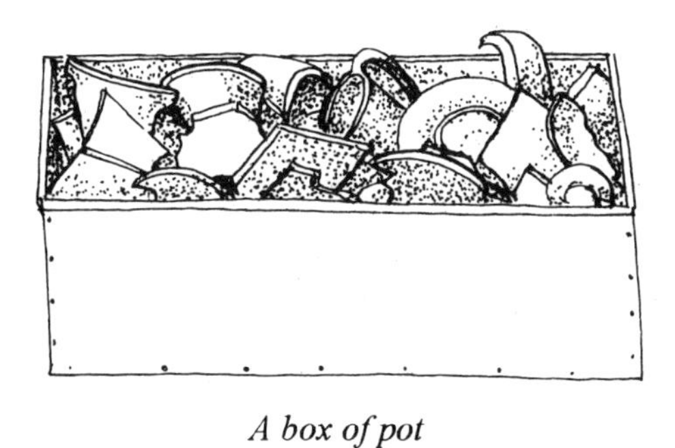

A box of pot

9

'Getting toned up for tonight's show, old man?' asked Roger, settling himself in the basket chair by the side of my bed. 'Hell, you look as if you've had a hard day. Cheer up! Think of your coming triumph as the Old Man of Grasmere.'

I groaned. 'Read that,' I said, waving a dejected paw at Peter's note.

He read it with some difficulty. 'What's aunt Emmy's pull?' he asked.

'Money. Widow of a plastic tycoon, or something. Has the bank practically bursting at the seams. And she's a double-headed old battleaxe into the bargain. When she says jump, Peter takes off like a pole-vaulter.'

'Mercenary beggar.'

'Only in the cause of science. He's hoping she'll finance another season's digging at Great Dodmanham. So he's got to hover round her bed.'

'Puts you in a bit of a spot, though,' said Roger, thoughtfully. 'Not your fault, of course, but old Subcourse won't see it like that. He'll say you should have chosen an archæologist without aunts, or at least shanghaied him before the course started. Still, you'll be able to cobble up a lecture. You've got the pots, you've got the notes, and you've got about a hundredweight of assorted books.'

'Oh, yeah? You can see what Peter's fist is like. Little lines of sportive words run wild. A sort of action writing. And when'll I have time to read the books? Damn it all, I've hardly got time to read the chapter headings.'

'You make too much of it, old boy,' said Roger soothingly. 'It's quite simple. All you have to do is whip through the notes, pick out the main headings, and list every ruddy piece of jargon you can find - you know, Levalloisian, Kitchen Midden cultures, notched tangs, perverted rims, and so on. String it together with a page or two from each of these tomes, and there you are. Oh, and drop a few Biddles and Leakeys about, just to show who your buddies are. Easy. It'll be absolute nonsense, of course, but who's to know? They won't remember any of it. They won't even understand it. But they'll think it's a marvellous lecture.'

'They might,' I said, 'but somehow I doubt it. It's not my style. They'd spot the fake in an instant. And anyhow, they don't want me, they want a real live archæologist, a pothunter, a bloody gravedigger, with muck in his fingernails.'

'Isn't there anyone else you could get?'

'Not at this short notice. Tittles-Hall might do it, but he's in London until to-morrow morning - only getting back in time to take us round his Roman villa, in fact. Oh, hell! I suppose I'll have to knock up something for them.'

'Ah, don't worry. You don't want to let a little thing like a missing lecturer upset you. A cool, calm head is all you need.'

'And an imbecilic friend who'll stand in. Wait a minute,' I said, feeling like Archimedes as the water began to slop over, 'wait a minute. What are you doing tomorrow? Aren't you free till lunchtime?'

'What? Can't remember, old boy.'

'Like hell you can't,' I said, taking a copy of his syllabus from the dressing-table. 'Here you are. Wednesday morning. "Free Morning".'

'Yes, but damn it all!' said Roger, shooting up from his chair and upsetting my bedside table. 'Sorry. Bulb's bust. The lamp's, not mine, you goon. Look, I've got a hell of a lot of preparation to do, and besides, I don't know a word of archæology. Not a word.'

'Liar. And irrelevant. You can have the notes, and the books. You told me yourself what to do with them, and you're always on the crack about your fantastic powers of assimilation. Well, here's a real chance to flex them. And remember,' I went on, seeing that he was still unenthusiastic, 'that if I've got to mug up a lecture, I shan't have time to put on a Wordsworth act tonight.'

'Blackmail,' said Roger, gloomily. 'You hound.'

'Call it a *quid pro quo.*'

'Yes, but dash it all, there's a world of difference between reading a few lousy lines of poetry and giving a whacking great lecture. And they know I'm not an archæologist. Subcourse does, for a start. And the Gorlestones. And Slimy Joe. And don't, for God's sake, suggest that I disguise myself as Peter Wood-Norton. They probably know him. His mug is in the local rag practically every week in the digging season, holding up some beastly relic or other. No, sorry, old chap,' said Roger, his voice firming up with regret, 'I'd like to help, but -'

'But wait,' I said, as he began to edge towards the door. 'I have a plan.'

'Odds bods!'

'Odds bods indeed. You can't impersonate Peter, of course, but what about - well, say Humphrey Godwick?'

'Never heard of him, old man.'

'Neither has the audience. And neither,' I said, frankly, 'have I. So that means no-one will know what he looks like.'

'Yes, but they know what *I* look like.'

'Not with a beard and glasses.'

'You're not suggesting that I take over your Wordsworth beard -'

'No, no, of course not. By the time I've finished with Wordsworth every hair of that beard will be imprinted in their minds for good. No, there's another in the cupboard.'

'Not,' said Roger, paling, 'that forked thing? Damn it all, it'll make me look like Old Nick.'

'So much the better. I confidently expect no small amount of *diablerie* in your performance, and you may as well look the part. How about a dramatic entrance? I'll apologise for Peter's absence, and say that instead we're going to hear Humphrey Godwick. I mean, dammit, with a name like that they'll be expecting some mild old coot with a drip on the end of his nose. And then - sensation! the door blasts open, and in strides this handsome young demi-god with the forked beard, fire flashing from his ice-blue eyes -'

'Thanks, old chap,' said Roger, 'but I don't think it's really me. Or rather, it's completely me, except for the beard. If I've got to wear that forked abomination I'm going to get as far away from my real character as possible. What about something Dickensian? A sort of Bronze Age Fagin? A stoop and a limp - grubby, arthritic hands - a wart or two - some beastly but fascinating habit, like picking my ears with a ball-point pen or using an old sock as a handkerchief. Yes, there are distinct possibilities in this.'

I could see that his imagination was smouldering, if not exactly fired.

'H'm,' I said, beginning to have misgivings. 'Don't go too far, will you? Be careful. There'd be all hell to pay if you were unmasked.'

'And the same goes for you tonight, Bill, old friend. By the way, here's the Book of Books, with marked passages.' He handed me a scruffy copy of Wordsworth's Collected. 'I'll take the Wood-Norton notes. I shan't have time for the books. I say, old chap, you might glance through them and mug up a bit of superficial knowledge. A few technical terms, that sort of thing. They'll come in useful for questions, and I might dry up. You never know. Now, about tonight. You, as Morley Swanton, will have to appear from outside. I thought Borwich station would be good cover. Not that we'll actually go there, of course. I'll nip off in your car, rendezvous with you halfway down the drive, and when we reach a secluded spot you can change into the clobber. I'll get it into the car. Then we can drive back, with Morley Swanton beside me on the front seat. And after the lecture we reverse the process. Simple, but masterly.'

I nodded gloomily.

'We'll have to skip supper, but that can't be helped,' he went on. 'I've got some fodder that we can get stuck into afterwards. Midnight feast in the dorm and all that. By the way, your lot have been invited to the show.'

'Oh, ah,' I said, without enthusiasm. 'What time shall I meet you?'

'Seven. On the third stroke precisely. All right? Good. Pip-pip.'

Ten minutes' work in a murky woodlet a couple of miles from Great Mardle produced a new Hautbois, up to his ears in whiskers. I felt like some shy creature of the forest, peering at the outside world through a thicket. Even the noble brow was overhung by a bosky wig. This was all to the good, for I felt most strongly that the fewer of my characteristic features that were exposed the better. Liberal use of mascara had given me another black eye to match my natural one. Below the neck there was less cause for satisfaction. The coat was far too big; my paws cowered in its sleeves like a pair of hermit crabs, and the tails had already struck up a passionate, lingual love-affair with the tops of my knee-boots. On the other hand, the cut-away front left me feeling a bit underdressed, for the breeches fitted like a coat of paint.

'They may swallow me as Morley Swanton,' I said, breaking the awestruck silence, 'or they may not. I knew I'd be running the risk of being nicked on a charge of impersonation. What I didn't bargain for is the much more likely one of indecent exposure.'

'You worry too much, old fellow,' said Roger. 'No-one's going to bother about that. Dash it all, everyone knows that Regency breeches were well cut.'

'Cut,' I said, wincing as I made a trial move, 'is the exact word. There's a damn good chance that halfway through the evening my voice will suddenly shoot up a couple of octaves.'

'Then we'll switch you to Dorothy's letters. The essential thing is to keep your head in a situation like this.'

'It's not my head I'm worried about.'

'Ah, come on, you'll be all right. You look splendid.'

'Frankly, I feel like some zoological freak. If I walked past the Natural History Museum they'd whip me inside and have me stuffed in a jiffy. And as for looking like Wordsworth -'

'Not the point, old chap,' said Roger. 'At least you won't be identified as W. Hautbois, unless it's by your legs and what-not.'

'Come, Barton-Bendish,' I said, coldly. 'You grow coarse. Shall we return to Great Mardle, or do you want to call the whole thing off?'

I won't pretend I enjoyed that short ride. Quite apart from the spiritual agony, those confounded breeches wouldn't allow me to bend more than a few degrees, and I had to prop myself against the front seat in a diagonal position. With Roger driving like a madman we could have been mistaken for the getaway car of a smash-and-grab raid on Madame Tussaud's. There was, fortunately, no welcoming committee as we drew up at the front door, but to satisfy any hidden observers we dismounted in the characters of the aged Master and the respectful young acolyte. As a matter of fact I needed all the help I could get, for the breeches were so constricting that my valetudinarian totter to the door on Roger's arm was not so much a truimph of characterisation as the best I could manage in the circumstances. We went straight to the lecture-room. Roger stood me up against a marble pillar just outside the door and went in. We had arranged a little spot of business to make my entry at once more dramatic and less dangerous. The room was blacked out; Roger was to say a few of the well-chosen about his distinguished guest, and on the cue 'Ladies and gentlemen, Morley Swanton as Mr. William Wordsworth' all the lights except a small reading lamp were to be switched off and I would make my entrance to the startled applause of the company. This triumph of careful planning would, Roger considered, give another dent to the impressionable Dr Subcourse.

Leaving out the question of whether anything less than a nuclear warhead would dent Dr Subcourse, I was rather dubious about the scheme. And as if to confirm my doubts something went wrong at the very start. The essential point in the timing of the operation was that I should be able to hear the cue, and to this end Roger had left the door ajar; but before he even began to speak some officious bastard inside the room jumped up and shut it. It was a solid construction of Honduras mahogany, and effectively soundproof. For about a minute I hesitated, hoping that Roger would realise that it was shut and either open it or raise his voice at the vital moment to a majestic trump that would split the panels and summon me to judgement. But when it remained closed and silent I decided that it was up to me to do something about it. Edging forward, I grasped the handle, meaning to open the door a crack and hear what was going on.

One of the disadvantages of being a man of quick, firm decisions, Roger explained to me afterwards, is that there are occasions when a quick, firm, decisive act merely accentuates a maladjustment in the timing of a combined operation. Coming to the annunciatory part of his prologue, he glanced at the door to make sure that I was hovering and was horrified to see that it was shut. He couldn't tell whether I could hear the cue or not, but he knew that the door would certainly have to be open before I could come through it, and it struck him that opening it in a flamboyant, flunkeylike way would serve the purpose of a cue. So he strode across and twitched it open, announcing as he did so 'Morley Swanton as Mr W-'

The illiam died on his lips, killed by the shock of seeing his distinguished guest enter the room horizontally and at a speed approaching mach two. I'd been caught off balance, but no more than a slight stagger would have resulted if my damned oversize cuff hadn't snagged on the handle and catapulted me into the room. Fortunately there was a clear space beyond the door, but my touch-down was inelegant and painful. Willing hands helped me up and propped me against the wall, and someone brought me a glass of water. It was meant kindly, no doubt, but I'd had no practice at drinking through a beard and a straw would have been invaluable. The small amount of liquid that eventually reached my mouth tasted as if it had passed through an old horsehair-and-flock mattress. After a while I recovered sufficiently to take stock of the damage, and found it surprisingly little. The coat was dusty but unharmed, and the breeches were unsplit. Even more of a relief was the fact that everyone was treating me as Morley Swanton, and this, mind you, in an audience that included many of my own students. Dr Bawdeswell brought up chairs by the dozen, Dr Subcourse asked me at least five times if I'd like him to get a doctor, and Mrs Gorlestone, not to be left out of anything, offered me the use of her son's bed. I declined everything with growing vigour, and after about five minutes they all returned to their seats and left us to get on with it.

It's difficult for me to say how the performance went. In plan it was a series of long readings from the bard, each prefaced by a short introduction from Roger. He did his bit admirably, and I got through my readings without interruption, but the technical difficulties were so great that I simply hadn't any attention to spare for observation of the audience. I solved the problem of movement by taking up my stand behind the reading-desk and refusing to budge, so that Roger had to speak from the side-lines. This meant that my vital parts not only were saved a great deal of wear and tear but were also removed from the view of most of the audience. But the rest of it wasn't so easy. Roger had provided me with a Victorian edition of the poems that had been printed by a crank of the Lord's-Prayer-on-a-postage-stamp school, and though my eyesight is pretty good I felt at times like a man trying to read microfilm without the usual enlarger. The enormous cuffs of the coat got in the way of the action, too, and every time I turned a page I had to haul in a couple of yards of sleeve. But the hazardous passage of the text was by no means over when it reached the eye. It had to be transmuted into sound. Now, there were two main requirements. One, I had to disguise my natural voice, which had a noticeable Borshire accent; and two, I had to produce something that would be credible as an aged Morley Swanton impersonating the great Lake Poet. The aged part was fairly simple; the Cumbrian flavour not so. In fact, what came out was a hybrid, mainly Welsh but with varying strains of the West Riding, Dorset, and Cockney, with an occasional waft from the back streets of Glasgow. Moreover, as the evening wore on it became increasingly clear that

Roger, as chief beard-sticker, had used far too much gum, and as it dried and hardened I felt as if my lips were being squeezed into a particularly powerful elastic band. This probably accounted for the involuntary whistle that made occasional appearances in the later poems.

With all these difficulties the text suffered a few startling mutilations. An unusually severe struggle with the cuff, for instance, caused me to turn over two pages at once, thereby joining the front half of The Daisy to the rear half of The Sexton. Nobody seemed to notice. The uncontrollable accent led to such mutations as 'O Cuckoo! shall I call thee bad, Or but a wandering vice?' and the interesting but in the event disappointing title 'The Solitary Raper'. And once when, through familiarity, I let my attention wander a little from the text the result was disconcerting; coming to the sonnet beginning 'Two voices are there' I thought joyfully to myself 'Blast, I know this one' and, lifting my head, gave them J. K. Stephens' parody, which begins with the same words but goes on to compare Wordsworth, in certain moods, to an old half-witted sheep. Roger turned it neatly by asking if anyone had spotted that it wasn't by Wordsworth. No-one had.

An hour and a half of this left the audience in somewhat of a coma. We asked for questions, but few came. The nastiest, predictably, was Mrs Gorlestone's.

'Mr. Swanton,' she said, 'I have always understood that Wordsworth was a clean-shaven man. Perhaps you could tell us why you are wearing a beard?'

For a moment I reeled; then inspiration came.

'Madam,' I fluted, drawing myself up, 'do you expect me to shave it off for a single performance?'

'Mr. Swanton has a train to catch,' said Roger, stepping in quickly, 'so I'm afraid we must bring this session to a close. I would, sir, like to thank you...'

And so, it appeared, would Dr Subcourse. At some length. After about five minutes Roger, with a magnificently selfless gesture, ostentatiously looked at his watch. The doctor took the hint.

'I am reminded,' he said, 'that our distinguished guest has a train to catch. I shall say no more, therefore, except to tender him our hearty thanks for a most interesting evening. Thank you, Mr Swanton.' And he clapped his hands twice, as gently as if he were holding an egg in them.

'And now,' he went on, as the applause died down and the audience began to stir, 'I shall do myself the honour of offering my services to you as chauffeur for your journey to the station.'

'That's all arranged, Dr Subcourse,' said Roger, quickly. 'I'm taking him back.'

'No, no. I insist. You have had a hard evening, Mr Barton-Bendish, and you have earned the right to take your ease. Moreover, I have to drive to Borwich tonight, and it will mean only a slight diversion to call at the station. By the way, Mr Barton-Bendish, I was under the impression that you have no car here?'

'I haven't. But I can borrow Bill's - Mr Hautbois.'

'Ah. As a matter of interest, where *is* Mr Hautbois tonight?'

'He had to go and see a sick aunt,' said Roger, without hesitation.

'Then he will have taken his car.'

'No. She sent a taxi.'

'Goodness me,' said Dr Subcourse. 'Well, sir,' he went on, turning to me, 'I have no wish to hasten your departure, but if the train you intend to catch is the 9.55 for London I think we ought to make our way to my car. You have no bag? Well, let me take your arm.'

He took it. I gave Roger an appealing glance, but I knew it was hopeless. Short of laying one on the Subcourse nut and making off with me into the night there was nothing he could do. As we tottered through the corridors I comforted myself with the thought that the doctor hadn't, apparently, penetrated my disguise, and all I would have to do on the journey to the station would be to maintain my impersonation. And the easiest and most convincing way to act as an ancient literary man would after a hard evening would be to go to sleep.

The car ride was, in fact, deceptively peaceful. Dr Subcourse installed me in the back seat, and I got some relief from the breeches by wedging my shoulders into one corner and reclining obliquely across the width of the car. I closed my eyes and started a few deep breathing exercises, and after a gambit or two had gone unanswered the doctor gave up the attempt to make conversation. When we drew up at the station I allowed him to wake me and help me out; then I thanked him, shook hands, and bade him good night and a safe journey, my boy. My idea was that he should take the hint and drive off, but the officious blighter insisted on accompanying me into the station, leading me through the booking-hall, past the refreshment room and the gents', and up to the barrier; and what's more he was babbling all the time about a short study of fifteenth-century papal bulls that he was bringing out in the autumn. He wanted me to see him all right with the London reviewers. I said I'd do what I could. What I really longed to do was push him under a train, but to accomplish this I would have had to get him on to the platform, and neither of us, of course, had a ticket. In fact, I was expecting him to leave me at the barrier, where I would hover for a few minutes until he'd disappeared and then sneak back to Great

Mardle. But instead of oiling off like a gentleman he insisted, in the teeth of my protests, that he would see me safely seated. At the barrier I went through the motions of searching my pockets for my return ticket, but no-one seemed to be surprised when I couldn't find it. The collector, who obviously regarded Dr Subcourse as my keeper, said that as the train was about to leave I'd better be shoved on it and pay my fare to the inspector, and so, half a minute later, I found myself seated in a first-class compartment, watching the platform slide away at the beginning of what was scheduled as a high-speed journey to London with only one intermediate stop.

The immediate problem was that my pockets were as empty as a politician's promise. I made a formal search, of course, but all I found was a couple of matchsticks, four throat pastilles of the kind favoured by Caruso, and a wodge of used chewing-gum. And to make matters worse I suddenly realised that I was hungry and thirsty. I'd had no supper, and my stomach was as empty as my pockets. I tried one of the pastilles; it tasted old and tired, like a piece chipped off the india-rubber bedstead exhibited at the Crystal Palace in 1851. Unsatisfied, I wandered along the corridor to sample the quality of the washbasin tap. As I emerged from the little room, full of water and whatever noxious chemical they put in it to discourage first-class hydromaniacs from drinking the train dry, I noticed that we were slowing down. I was just saying to myself that I supposed yet another of those diesel monsters had broken down when it struck me that if it stopped altogether I might well be advised to alight.

It did. I alighted. Being the middle of summer it wasn't yet pitch dark, and someone, possibly the guard, saw me and let out an official yell. We had stopped in a cutting which, fortunately, ran through a small wood. I went up the bank like a hare and in a matter of seconds was crouching in the cover of the trees. A moment later the engine honked and moved on, taking the train with it.

I sat still for a few minutes, partly to get my breath, partly to work out where in Borshire I was, and partly to carry out a survey of my fabric. The sudden sprint, I discovered, had been altogether too much for my breeches. The central seam had had a nervous breakdown, and I was now wearing a garment that would have done admirably for a couple of one-legged ballet-dancers but was definitely unsuitable for any normal male. I must, therefore, keep well away from the public eye, and slink back to Great Mardle by way of woods and by-roads. I didn't know exactly where I was, but I worked out that if I kept my face to the west it wouldn't be long before I came upon some feature that would tell me approximately how far I was from Mardle.

And so it proved. I hadn't been walking more than ten minutes when I came upon a church that I knew, and after that it was plain sailing. The only person I saw was a solitary cyclist, and he, understandably, didn't stop to investigate the strange figure that wandered into the beam of his headlight. I got back to Great Mardle just after midnight. Someone - Roger, I guessed - had left the door on the latch, so I didn't have to break and enter a second time. Safely in my room, I found a flask of tea, a pork pie, two doughnuts, a lemon curd tartlet, and a banana arranged tastefully on my dressing-table. I wolfed the lot, dewhiskered myself, unbreeched, washed, toileted, and went to bed, taking a few of the archæological tomes with me for a little light reading.

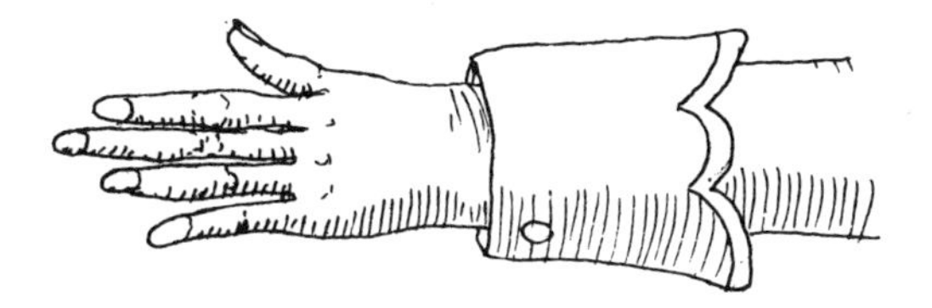

A damned oversize cuff

10

I was awakened by thunder. At least, at the moment of waking I thought it was thunder, but it turned out to be metaphorical rather than meteorological - a hammering on the door, in fact. It was accompanied by the voice of Dr Subcourse, calling on me to open up. A quick squint at my watch told me that it was a quarter past nine. I had overslept - but not enough, surely, to warrant a visit from the Boss and his thugs? Fortunately I'd locked the door last night as a precaution against the chance discovery of my Wordsworth gear, so they couldn't get in without breaking it down.

'Just a minute!' I called. 'I'm dressing.'

But to make myself decent proved to be a minor problem. A gruff request for some action, coming this time not from the doctor but from his side-kick, Scarface Gorlestone, told me that this was no mere show-a-leg call. Something big was in the wind, and I had it in a flash. The corset! The doctor had promised unpleasant action yesterday morning if it were not returned, and now the deadline had been reached. They had evidently decided to search the rooms, and no-one, but no-one, would be exempt. They'd probably begun with the lair of the Gorlestone herself. I'd have to hide the blasted thing, and a glance round the room and a few moments' thought told me that the only safe place was next to the skin. So I slipped behind the wardrobe curtain to get it.

It wasn't there. I searched the wardrobe frantically, but it simply wasn't there. I came out and sat on the bed. Where the hell was the thing? Dismissing the possibility that I could have disposed of it in my sleep, I was left with the presumption that some other hand, friendly or unfriendly, had removed it. Who knew about it? Katherine, Iris, and possibly Roger. Any of these could have taken it, but Iris was the only one who knew, definitely, that it was hanging up in the wardrobe, and who had the positive goodwill towards me to take such trouble to save me from a fate worse than death.

Another fit of cursing from the other side of the door reminded me that there were guests without, and that I was still left with a body to dispose of, viz., the Wordsworth outfit. Here again the only safe place was about the person, so I whipped into the breeches, the boots, and the coat, and covered the whole thing with a pair of ordinary trousers and a massive turtle-necked sweater, which also provided accommodation for the wig and beard in one of its enormous dewlaps. Then, sweating, I opened the door.

I hadn't expected it to be a pleasant visit, and it wasn't. They seemed to take my delay in opening the door as a sure sign that I had something to hide, and brushing aside my protests they searched the room from floor to ceiling. At least, Dick Gorlestone did the actual searching (very reluctantly, I thought) while his mother and Dr. Subcourse stood by and directed him. And from their side-footed remarks I gathered that, far from being well down in the betting-list of suspects, Ben Adhem Hautbois's name led all the rest. It was the way I'd bragged about my exploits in the house of the grackles-fancier, I found, that had put them wise to my lack of respect for the laws of property, and so when the time came to swoop they swooped on Room D, Floor Three, confident that they would catch me in possession of the looted article. There was some divergence, interestingly enough, between them on the nature of the offence. The doctor seemed to think that it was a minor crime, indicative of some weakness in the moral fibre and showing an insufficient grasp of the *meum-tuum* principle, perhaps, but basically a tasteless prank that merited, at the most, a sentence of seven days in the jug without the option. Mrs.Gorlestone's interpretation was more sinister. It wasn't so much that I was the most likely person in Great Mardle to snitch a corset, she implied, as that I couldn't keep my hands off the things. No corset, roll-on, girdle, or suspender-belt or panty-hose could count itself safe once I got my nose to the trail. If I were allowed to roam unchecked, in a couple of days no woman in the place would have a stitch of underwear left.

And dammit! she wasn't a bit put out when Dick turned the last stone and reported that the joint was clean. Oh ho! she snorted, so he's passed it to his accomplice, has he, the yellow-bellied liverfluke, or words to that effect. And when I asked who she thought my accomplice was, she said that Southwood girl, of course. We'd been sniggering together ever since the beginning of the course, and had taken a gross delight in making insulting remarks. Moreover, she had some suspicion that our relations were irregular. We had absented ourselves from the coach on Monday afternoon, and had arrived home with our arms about each other and some cock-and-bull story on our lips. There'd been every opportunity for misbehaviour. Where was the girl Southwood's room? Next door? Aha! She thought so. Come, Dr Subcourse.

They went out, and I followed. It wasn't at all likely that Katherine had the corset, of course, but if by a singular chance it was she and not Iris that had lifted it the least I could do would be to claim that I'd planted it on her. But it was much more likely that Iris had got it, and I'd probably have to do the like service for her. In any case, I was still chief suspect.

Katherine was waiting for us. I discovered afterwards that everyone had got the stand-by-your-beds order, and such was its force that Florence Babingley and Meribell Twyford stood by theirs conscientiously till lunch-time, unaware that the search had been called off some three hours before. But that's to anticipate. Katherine, as I say, was waiting for us, having probably heard all that had been said in my room. She certainly didn't get any other warning, for Mrs Gorlestone, her pressure raised to something like 230 lbs p.s.i., just steamed in without the customary knock.

'Richard!' she cried. 'Search this room.'

Richard hadn't appeared any too happy when searching mine, and now, faced with the prospect of going through a collection of female knicknackeries, he looked distinctly rebellious. And Katherine objected, too. Mrs Gorlestone, she suggested, would be the best person to do the searching; a man would have the embarrassment of holding up each article for identification, but the owner of the missing garment would, presumably, know her own cami-knickers. She'd be obliged, too, if the men would leave the room while the search was in progress. To this Mrs Gorlestone counter-objected. Richard could wait outside, yes, but Dr Subcourse, as Director and a married man, was fully entitled to be there.

'As for this young man,' she went on, drawing the hem of her skirt away from me, 'I am convinced that he was concerned with the disappearance of the article, and I wish him to be present when it is discovered. I wish to confront him with it.'

'Lucky him,' said Katherine.

'Miss Southwood!'

'Well, it's up to you, Mrs Gorlestone, of course. It's your underwear. But I don't see why he should be confronted with mine.'

'Really, young woman, do you mean to be impertinent?'

'Oh, no. Just modest.'

'Modest!' snorted Mrs Gorlestone. 'Richard! Wait outside. You, Mr Oh-bwah, will stay, but in deference to Miss Southwood's modesty - real or assumed - I expect you to exhibit some delicacy and avert your gaze.'

'Certainly,' I said, 'if Dr Subcourse will do the same.'

'Dr Subcourse is a gentleman.'

'Ah,' I said. 'That does make a difference.'

'Might I ask,' said Katherine, gently, 'why you think the garment, whatever it is, is in my room?'

'They think,' I said, before another jaw could move, 'that I snitched it while on a midnight prowl, and when the heat was turned on I simply passed it to you.'

'Why me?'

'My closest known associate.'

'It has been abundantly evident from the first,' said Mrs Gorlestone, severely, 'that you and Oh-bwah share a somewhat juvenile sense of humour. I myself have seen you sniggering together more than once. There have been impertinent remarks. Most impertinent. And it is suggestive that your room is adjacent to his. *Most* suggestive.'

'And what do you mean by that?' asked Katherine. There was a distinct hardening in her tone.

'I shall not be more explicit. I *need* not be more explicit.'

'What do you mean about our rooms being adjacent?'

'I mean exactly what I said,' snapped Mrs Gorlestone. 'The fact that your rooms are adjacent is suggestive. Most suggestive.'

'Suggestive of what?'

'I'm sure I need say no more than that.'

'You mean,' said Katherine, slowly, 'that you think we've been sharing a bed?'

'Young woman,' said Mrs Gorlestone, drawing herself up as if she'd had a sharp nip in the kidneys, 'I am not now concerned with your morals. They do not interest me. But there has been much more than a suggestion of the improper about your relations with Mr Oh-bwah, and that *does* concern me, for he is responsible for the running of this section of the Summer School. There have been complaints that his diligence has been affected by the attention he is paying you, and I think that these complaints are justified. I have only to mention the time you spent together on Monday afternoon, at Swinesthorpe, when Mr Oh-bwah should have been attending to his work. It was irregular, most irregular. There was every opportunity for misbehaviour, and the ridiculous story invented to explain your absence is merely proof that something improper occurred. And it was reported to me only last night that you have been seen coming from Mr Oh-bwah's room. It may, of course, have been an innocent visit. I do not know. But I shall not, I will not countenance even the appearance of impropriety, and your affair with this young man has passed far beyond the bounds of mere appearance. I am convinced of that.'

'Oh, yes?' said Katherine. Her voice was cool enough, but her cheeks were pretty red. 'Then perhaps you can explain why I'm having an affair with Mr Hautbois when in fact I'm engaged to someone else?'

'What?' I cried.

Mrs Gorlestone gave me a look of contempt. 'Mr Oh-bwah appears to be unaware of your engagement. Perhaps you could enlighten him - and the rest of us - by telling us the name of your fiancé?'

'I really don't think that's any of your business, Mrs Gorlestone,' said Katherine, slowly.

Mrs Gorlestone snorted. 'Just as I thought! Another fabrication!'

'Oh, all right, then. It's Tony Saham.'

'Mr Saham? Professor Saham's son?'

'Yes.'

Mrs Gorlestone drew in her chin and looked thoughtful. She was undoubtedly in a dilemma. An attachment to the utterly respectable Saham would confer a certain respectability to Katherine, but on the other hand it would put the mockers on her theory about Bonnie Southwood and Clyde Hautbois, purloiners of gentlewomen's underwear. But she could hardly admit that she had been wrong.

'I fear,' she said at last, 'that nowadays an engagement means nothing. Nothing. Indeed, the bond of marriage itself is often insufficiently strong to restrain the coarse instincts of a certain class of person.'

This was getting a bit thick.

'Look,' I said, sharply, 'I don't mind what you say about me, but please leave Miss Southwood out of it. She's got nothing to do with all this. She's done nothing to be ashamed of. You're talking as if she were a common drabbletailed strumpet.'

This curious expression which, no doubt through some associative kink, sprang more or less unbidden to my lips, had landed one Peter Day in the Consistory Court in 1632 on a charge of slander, and even in the liberated and enlightened twentieth century it caused no little stir. The doctor responded with another rarity, the academic tut-tut, followed by a pursing of the lips and a slow shaking of the head, as if he were being gently throttled. Mrs Gorlestone stepped smartly away from me, bringing her right buttock into sharp contact with the corner of the washbasin.

'Mr Oh-bwah!' she cried, her voice full of pain and anguish. 'I consider that a most disgusting term.'

'I fully concur,' said the doctor. 'It is certainly *not* an expression that one should use in mixed company, Hautbois. It implies that Miss Southwood is, ah, little better than, ah, a woman of the streets.'

'Well, actually,' said Katherine. We all looked quickly at her. 'Actually, it sounded to me more like a rather jolly little bird of the wayside and woodland. Mrs Gorlestone, I'm sure you're not comfortable. Would you like a chair?'

'No, thank you,' said Mrs Gorlestone, stiffly. 'Miss Southwood, I must ask you to permit us to search your room.'

'Go ahead.'

'Miss Southwood, I feel we owe you something of an apology,' said Dr Subcourse, a few minutes later. Mrs Gorlestone was at that moment tackling her last hope, a drawer so small that even a couple of aspirins would have felt unpleasantly overcrowded in it. 'The article does not appear to be in your possession, and I am sorry that you should have been subjected to this - ah - indignity.'

'Thank you.'

'Well,' I said, drawing a deep breath, 'It's nice to be back in the ranks of the innocent. I take it we *are* cleared of all suspicion?'

Mrs Gorlestone closed the drawer with a bang.

'Certainly not!' she snorted.

'But the thing wasn't in my room,' I pointed out, 'and it isn't here. If it's still in our possession, we must have eaten it. Perhaps a spot of vivisection, or a stomach-pump - no? Or perhaps Katherine's wearing it? Are you sure you wouldn't like her to strip?'

'Come, doctor,' said the old girl, picking up a handbag that was large enough to hold a full set of plumber's tools, 'there are still many rooms to be searched.'

'I shall speak to you later, Hautbois,' said the doctor, turning to go.

'Just a moment,' I said. 'I don't want to spoil your fun, but it's now a quarter to ten, and I've got to collect my speaker from Borwich station. He's due to begin lecturing at a quarter past. Do you think you could postpone your investigations? I want all my students to hear him. He's a most exceptional man.'

This simple, businesslike request was undoubtedly the most effective thing I'd said that morning. The gentle hint that, even in the midst of my tribulations, I yet had time to think of my duty to Education and the APES stopped the baying corset-hounds in their tracks. They turned on me, but instead of the rending of flesh the air was filled with of-courses, students must-come-firsts, and thank-you-Mr Hautbois-for-reminding-us-of-the-times. I had, unwittingly, appealed to their best instincts. No doubt the old blood-lust would return, but for the moment the stern daughter of the voice of God had them both in a half-nelson. They hurried off, muttering about Orders for the Day.

'Well,' I said, as the thunder of hoofs died away, 'sorry you were let in for all that. The moral is, choose your friends with discretion. I'm glad that's over. What used to be called a *mauvais quart d'heure,* I believe.'

'More like twenty minutes,' she said, looking at her watch. 'By the way, I've got a message from your lecturer.'

'My *lecturer?* Peter Wood-Norton?'

'No, no. Humphrey Godwick.'

'What!'

'It's all right. He thought for some reason he could trust me. He said would you pick him up near the entrance gate at ten o'clock, as he's found a hut to change in and won't need to go to the green room. He said you'll recognise him by his beard.'

'That,' I said, gloomily, 'sounds as if he's done something really shocking to his appearance. Roger goes just a little bit too far, sometimes. I wonder if he's got the corset? If he has, we'll see it flying at half-mast from the flagpole, or something. But the chances are that it was Iris who lifted it from my room in the nick of time. You don't happen to know, do you?'

'I'm afraid that I haven't kept a log of Iris's movements,' she said, rather coldly. 'I can't say when, or how many times, she's been to your room.'

'Oh,' I said.

'And now,' she went on, 'do you mind leaving? I've got to change.'

'Oh, why? You look very nice as you are.'

'Oh.' She hesitated for a fraction of a second as she glanced at me. 'Well, it's comfort, not appearance, that bothers me. How any woman,' she went on, putting her hands on her waist and doing a sort of irritable wriggle, 'can wear these things for more than half-an-hour at a stretch I can't imagine. Stretch! It's more like plate armour. And knowing Mrs G., it's probably bullet-proof. Mr Hautbois, if you think you can stand there and *gawp* at me while I undress, you're mistaken. The door's just behind you. I'll close it when you've gone out.'

She did, too. *And* locked it.

A drabble-tailed strumpet

11

At the end of the drive a ghastly figure nipped out of the trees and raised a grimy claw.

'Going my way?' it inquired.

'God forbid!' I said with a shudder. 'And what the hell are you got up as? Jack the Ripper?'

'Sorry, old boy,' said Roger. 'Limited stocks in anything my size. Anyway, disguise and picturesqueness are the main objects.'

He was wearing a Victorian dinner-jacket, a dickey that had three finger marks and part of a footprint in one corner, hairy black plus-fours, red and orange check stockings, a pair of climbing boots, a long black cloak lined with red satin, and a stovepipe hat. In addition to the forked beard he had long grey muttonchop whiskers, a pair of eyebrows that could have been a couple of samples from the bag of a traveller in goatskin rugs, and an immense, greasy wig that hung lankly down to his shoulders. In his hand was an ash stick, freshly cut.

'You're banking on a vast suspension of disbelief, aren't you?' I asked.

'Credibility is relative,' said Roger, confidenfly. 'You, William, see me as Roger Barton-Bendish, dressed up. The APES will see me as Humphrey Godwick, the eccentric archæologist, a complete character, a real, living person. They won't question my identity. You see, they won't be expecting a fiddle. And this'll be something to tell their grandchildren about. They'll simply lap it up.'

I thought it was more likely that half of them would have fits and the other half would rocket out of the windows, but I kept this to myself. I didn't want to shake his confidence.

'By the way,' he said, getting into the car. 'I've solved the problem of how to dispose of the body after the lecture. You won't want to take me back to Borwich, will you, and I certainly don't want a lift from old Subcourse. So I've ordered a taxi for half-past eleven.'

'Good,' I said. 'Thanks. I only hope the driver's a man of strong character and temperàte habits.'

'Oh, that's all right. Friend of mine. Well, how did you get on last night with my lord Director?'

I told him.

'Golly!' he said in simple awe, as my terse narrative ended. 'I'm sorry about that, but I couldn't foresee that he'd whisk you off like a teenage heiress, could I? Anyway, you're back, and that's what matters. And what of the great search this morning?'

On this subject I was even terser.

'Old boy,' he said, 'these things are sent to try us. I say, hadn't we better be getting along? I've set the pots and things out in the lecture room, but I don't want to be late. I hope you've got a couple of learned questions up the spout, ready to fire off at the end? Well, once more into the breach, dear friend, once more, as the bishop said.'

Mrs Gorlestone and the doctor were waiting to greet the lecturer. I hopped out of the car to open the door for Roger, and so was in a good position to watch their faces as he emerged. It was worth the little extra effort. The Gorlestone jaw practically hit the marble step, beating the Subcourse chops by a whisker. I can't say I was surprised by this reaction. Roger looked terrible. He must have felt this too, and he did the only thing: he pitched right in.

'Dr Subcourse, Mrs Gorlestone, sure and I'm very pleased to meet yez,' he cried, starting at top A and sliding down a couple of octaves like a Cresta champion. 'And how are yez, yourselves? Sure and it's a terrible rough track from London, to be sure. It's bruising it is I have all over me poor body, be jabbers. And this young feller here, didn't he droive like the wind, so help me, and his old rattletrap bouncing all over the road? I tell yez, it's shaken to pieces I am. To pieces! Thank God and the Holy Mary, says I, thank God I've not got me specimens on me, or sure and it is they'd now be in pieces no bigger than a gnat's tooth.' He turned on me fiercely. 'And weren't you telling me they came last night, Hautbois? Spake up, man, for God's sake! Have ye a bone in your jaw, or some such foolery?'

I was, as a matter of fact, waiting for the end. I couldn't believe they'd swallow this. They both had superhuman maws, but to take this lot they'd need the jaw spread of a hippo.

But I was wrong. It was, I suppose, simply the putting into practice of the old adage, if you're going to tell a lie, make it a king-size one, that did it. Moreover, Roger's irritation with me was balm to their souls.

'I must apologise on behalf of British Rail and Mr Hautbois,' said the doctor, suavely extending a hand and a couple of teeth. 'Welcome to Great Mardle, Mr Wood-Norton.'

I'd forgotten, of course, to apprise him of the change of lecturers.

'Sure,' said Roger, before I could explain, 'Peter Wood-Norton's in Bognor, licking the boots of a sick aunt of his. Or is it Bath? But 'tis a good lad, sure enough, and it was only too pleased I was to fill in for him. Wasn't I knowing his mother well, for God's sake, and that before he was born? 'Tis a poor thing if you can't scratch a back or two, I say. Well, young feller, and do I have to introduce meself to these good people?'

I introduced him, numbly.

'Do you know Borshire well, Mr Godwick?' asked Mrs Gorlestone.

'Pretty well, pretty well. Pretty well,' said Roger, experiencing a temporary drying-up. He turned on me to help him out. 'Now then, young feller, where's me pot?'

I was trying to shut the car door. Something seemed to be jamming it, and investigation showed that it was the Godwick ash.

'Sure, then, is that me shillelagh?' said a voice like audible Irish stew. 'And isn't it a step I can't be stirring without it? Ye'll not be breaking it, ye rip? Ah! That's better. Now, doctor, and where would I find your lecture-room? After your good self, ma'am.'

They went in. Resisting the temptation to get back into the car and head for the hills, I followed. Roger, I noticed, had developed a spasmodic limp, and by some delicate trick of footwork made it appear as if his right leg were wooden.

If only he were a real archæologist, I reflected as we went up the stairs, all this wouldn't matter in the slightest. The public simply sees a little eccentricity in dress and manner as an indication of a disturbed mind. And conversely, if it doesn't expect old Willie the village idiot, who spends his time collecting queer-shaped stones, to dress to Saville Row standards or even, more than one day in three, to get his boots on the right feet, it won't look for much sharpness in the garb of a nutter who has *devoted his entire life* to digging up bits of broken pots and fitting them together. On the other hand, the public expects anyone who presents himself as an archæologist to be able to deliver a lecture that, however incomprehensible to the man in the street, will make at least a little sense to other pothunters, and this, I feared, was likely to prove Roger's Achilles heel. Anyone with a smattering of archæology would shoot him down in a matter of seconds, and even Dr Subcourse, who couldn't tell the difference between Stonehenge and a blood-orange, might be prompted to draw a few bows at a venture.

But for once luck was on our side. As soon as I'd introduced the speaker, Dr Subcourse rose, made his apologies, and left the room, bound for some coven of educational warlocks in Borwich. Then Mrs Gorlestone, with a few words of welcome and regret, got up and left. She didn't say where she was going, but that didn't bother me at the time. My hopes began to rise. A searching glance around the class revealed no serious, overt threat. Dr Bawdeswell, of course, could be relied upon to provide a few bloody-minded niggles, but I suspected that his knowledge of archæology had been gleaned from W. Runcton Holmes's *Highways and Byways of Borshire* (1906), cheap edn. 6/-, which I'd seen him flashing at people like a cigarette-case all through the course. There might, of course, be more than one secret archæologist amongst us, for the outward symptoms are not always clear and can be confused with, for example, debility, senility, mild alcoholism, or the first stages of paranoia. Moreover, the sensation caused by Roger's bizarre appearance had confused the issue, and I couldn't be absolutely certain that, for instance, the expression on Agnes Bintry's lemur-like countenance was not a look of intelligent and informed interest but simply the product of shock and a couple of large morning sips from the brandy-flask. This would be something that only time would tell.

In fact, before he'd been speaking for five minutes I was sure that only the girl Katherine and myself realised that he was dishing out the biggest load of codswallop ever seen outside Billingsgate. Mind you, it was good codswallop, prime stuff, and it kept all but a few compulsive sleepers from dozing off. It gripped. 'This sherd of coarse gritty ware,' Roger would say, holding up half a pot of dull brown stuff, 'is undoubtedly Ebbsfleet derived. Note the omphalos base and inward-sloping neck, and, be Jasus, it's carinated and banded with a debased lozenge sub-pattern into the bargain, so it is. From the late Hallstatt-La Tène hill fort at Muckham St. Mary, dug out from under me very eyes, and sure a lovely piece it is, with a foine style to it, just the sort of thing, I'm thinking, that Queen Boadicea, God rest her! would be drawing on for a little ointment for the poor legs of her when she came in, all tired and beflapped from a hard day scything down the Romans on the A11, or as they called it, *Stræta Undecim.'* Ripe stuff like this, combining scholarship and the common touch, couldn't fail to go over big. The fact that the pot in question was conspicuously labelled on the inside 'Medieval cooking pot, Borwich Gas Works site' was neither here nor there. As long as it was presented as something interesting and important the audience were happy. I, too, was not unpleased with the way things were going. The great point was that Humphrey Godwick was riding the crest of a wave of credibility. He didn't have to be accurate as well. I sat back and began to relax.

Relaxed too much, in fact, for I nodded off. I had had a hard night, remember. I was roused by the sound of Roger proposing, with typical aplomb, a vote of thanks to himself for his extremely interesting lecture, and by the time I'd realised where I was he was shoving all his papers into a folder and muttering about a meeting with Barry Cunliffe at two o'clock.

'Ah! There ye are, me bhoy!' he cried, as I hurried towards him. 'Hope ye enjoyed my little talk. Be James, and it's dry me throat is! A drop of the crayture would not be amiss. However, no time for that. Me chariot's waiting! Take care of me pots, ye rip. I'm off.' And he turned and belted off down the corridor, trailing clouds of Peter Wood-Norton's notes behind him. I followed, picking them up. By the time I got to the main door he was just a puff of blue taxi-smoke hanging above the drive.

'Ah, lovely bed!' I said, sinking down beside Katherine Southwood on the front seat of the coach that was to take us on the excursion. 'Sorry, not really a Freudian slip, just a phrase expressing relief at a narrow escape from a fate worse than death. Patty Colkirk has been keeping a seat for me. I explained to her -'

'Excuse me, that's my seat,' said an unpleasant voice just above me.

I looked up. The face was unpleasant too. Tony Saham.

'Oh, ah?' I said. 'Well, I'm sorry, but I've got to sit at the front.'

'What about that one?' he asked, pointing to a single immediately behind the driver.

'It's all yours,' I said, cordially. 'This one gives me a better view. Essential for tricky navigating.'

'Look,' he said, 'this is my seat. I was here first. I was here ten minutes before you came. Flaming hell! You've got a nerve. I only have to leave for a second to get my camera, and you pinch my seat.'

'Ah, that's life.'

'Look,' he snarled, leaning down, 'are you going to get out?'

'You mind them seats,' said the driver, unexpectedly. He was not, fortunately, the gorilla who had driven us to Swinesthorpe. 'I don't want them seats mucked up. Why don't you ask the young lady which on you she want?'

'Nothing to do with me,' said the girl. 'I've never seen either of them before.'

'Pull the other one,' said the driver. 'Why don't you toss for it?' He fumbled in his pocket and produced a coin. 'Here, Tarzan, catch!'

Saham, of course, dropped it. It rolled down the steps of the coach and on to the gravel. He followed and picked it up.

'All right,' he said, sullenly. 'Call.'

'Heads,' I said, hurrying out of the coach as he flipped it. I didn't trust him.

'Tails it is.'

'Excuse me, gentlemen,' said Dr Bawdeswell, squeezing past us and up the steps.

'My seat, I think,' said Saham, smirking.

I followed him back into the coach.

'Bloody hell!' he said. Dr Bawdeswell was sitting beside Katherine.

I pushed past him and secured the seat behind the driver. For a few moments Saham hesitated; then, giving it up as a bad job, he turned and went down the coach, looking for a seat. I snuggled down. I knew the only one to spare was next to Miss Colkirk.

'Drive on, cabby,' I said.

'What about my fifty pence?' he demanded.

'Here you are,' I said, giving him one of my own store. It had been worth it. 'Now ho for Hollcaster! Tuppence extra if you get there before nightfall.'

'This,' said Caradoc Tittles-Hall, Site Director of Hollcaster and Pothunter Extraordinary, holding up a lopsided lump of crockery, 'is, of course, a mere fragment, but the form is indubitably situlate, with a very low carination. Note also the open vandyke above the base. One is forced to compare it with *this'* - and he whipped another undistinguished chunk from the box by his left hip - 'which has a finger-tip impressed cordon about its constricted neck. On the other hand...'

I felt like making a finger-tip impressed cordon about *his* ruddy constricted neck. I'd hoped, against all reason and experience, that he wouldn't insist on giving us a lecture, and that if he did he'd confine himself to the roman site. But both hopes had proved to be vain. He was ranging far and wide over the sherds of Borshire, leaping among his cardboard boxes and producing assorted crooks like a demented conjuror. Feeling very grass-tempered, I sank down on the sward behind the shouldered-bucket shape and rough herring-bone pattern of Ada Mulbarton. A glazed look was apparent on the faces around me. The pots of Dr Tittles-Hall seemed to differ from the pots of Humphrey Godwick only in being far less interesting, and one could see that many of the audience were thinking that you could have too much of a good thing. In fact, a globular and basal-looped murmur was beginning to creep from the hoard of coarser types at the back, and at one point there was a crudely-modelled comment in the unmistakable Rinyo-Clacton accents of Dr Bawdeswell. The bulk of the APES, however, were victims of an interesting carp's-tongue complex, and the one person who might have made a deep incision in the lecture - Mrs Gorlestone - was far too U-butt to interrupt a man with a hyphen to his name. She sat on a small folding canvas stool slightly in front of me, a fine specimen of the hard, fairly coarse ware produced by the Deverel-Rimbury folk. Hæmatite, I noticed, had been applied to the upper part of her exterior surface, producing a glossy, rust-coloured appearance which was varied on the lightly-scored parts by traces of white inlay. The remains of two vertical perforated lugs were interesting. From time to time she cast an everted, flattened look at her son, who was sitting, knees clasped, by the side of a distinctly developed and biconical type - Iris Overy, no less. Iris was looking very fetching, in a skin-tight jersey with a very low carination and open vandyke, and a pair of jeans that displayed to perfection her dimpled or omphalos base. Beyond them, Katherine was lodged between that debased version of a continental Hallstatt type, Dr Bawdeswell, and Tony Saham. Of the three, only Katherine, with her upright, rounded body, small flat base, slender upstanding neck with simple beaded decoration, and smoothed, slightly burnished surface, seemed at all at ease. She actually gave the impression of enjoying Dr Tittles-Hall's lecture. A fine-gritted piece; why on earth did she want to go and get herself engaged to that young Samian waster? Now *there* was another neck that could do with a bit of constricting. I spent the last half-hour of the lecture in a circular to sub-triangular depression, which even a lozenge variant slipped to me from the bag-shaped chape of Patty Colkirk could not relieve.

Eventually Tittles-Hall ran out of pots, and after a quick nip round the actual site we moved on to the plastic beaker period. Lunch over, we embussed again. This time Saham made no mistake; he and Katherine shared the front seat, and I had to go behind the driver.

The last visit of the day was to Brattling Park to see some barrows - round, cup, bell, or long, I couldn't remember which. I hoped fervently that Peter Wood-Norton's confidence in Lord Brattling was not misplaced. Peter had arranged the details of the visit, but now I wished that I'd taken more interest in them. I didn't even know his lordship. I ought at least to have reminded him that we were coming. It was more than likely that he'd forgotten all about us, and was now speaking in the House or visiting his estate in Cornwall or lounging in the Bahamas. I descended from the coach in front of the white-brick façade of Brattling Hall with a certain amount of apprehension, and the lifeless look of the house did nothing to reassure me. Still, I might flush a butler or two. I stepped up to the main door and knocked. This producing no apparent result, I looked around for some other means of letting the inhabitants know that there was a waif on the doorstep. My eye fell upon a bell-pull in the shape of a brazen nymph. Decades of polishing by victorian housemaids had made her practically sexless, so I had no qualms about grasping her firmly by the torso and giving her a hearty yank. Previous experience with mechanical bells had led me to expect a clang like the collapse of the Tay Bridge, but all I got on this occasion was a thundering silence, the nymph herself, and about three feet of rusty wire which some coarse craftsman had attached to her buttocks. I was still trying to feed this wire back into the hole in the wall when the door opened, revealing a tallish, thin domestic. He certainly wasn't the butler; in fact, his general scruffiness led me to believe that he was something like the cook's widowed brother-in-law. The high spots of his week, no doubt, were taking the kitchen rubbish-bin to the Home Farm pigs and operating the plunger and rods on the blocked drain in the stone courtyard. By his look he didn't seem to think all that much of me, either.

'She seems to have come out,' I said, holding up the nymph.

He grunted and disappeared behind the door. A moment later the wire whipped back into the socket, taking with it the nymph and a small portion of my right thumb. The man reappeared.

'Yes?' he said.

'I've brought a party of historians,' I said, trying to strike a dignified note, 'to see Lord Barrow's brattlings.'

'What?'

'Lord Brattling's barrows, I mean.'

He looked at me with a gleam of interest. 'You must be Mr Hautbois,' he said. 'I've heard about you.'

I could make nothing of this. I had my little niche in Borshire historical circles, of course, but I was far from notorious. I couldn't see how this chap could have heard of me, unless some whisper of the events at Great Mardle had drifted his way. Was he some ragged scion of the Mardle domestic grapevine?

'Mr Oh-bwah,' said Mrs Gorlestone, rudely interrupting my reverie, 'my members are getting impatient. I have told them that they may get out of the charabanc. Why is there such a delay?'

'Well, I had a slight accident with the bell-pull,' I said, indicating the nymph.

She gave the figure a censorious glance. 'Really? Well, that is scarcely the point. We have an appointment with Lord Brattling, my man,' she went on, addressing the varlet in the doorway. 'Please inform him that the A.P.E.S. party has arrived. Well, man! Why do you not go?'

'You must be Mrs Millstone,' he said.

If she'd have been armed with anything more lethal than a handbag those would have joined the deathless roll of Famous Last Words. As it was, it was touch and go whether or not he got half a hundredweight of alligator in the gizzard.

'My name,' she said, 'is Gorlestone.'

'Ah,' he said. 'I once knew a man called Bladder.'

'You are most insolent! I shall certainly report you to Lord Brattling. Now I should be *obliged* if you would tell him that I should like to see him.'

'Right-ho,' he said. 'Wait here.'

He closed the door. Three seconds later it opened again, to reveal the same nondescript figure.

'Mrs Gorlestone, Mr Hautbois,' he said, extending a paw. 'Welcome to Brattling Park!'

For a moment I actually felt sorry for Mrs Gorlestone. I mean, there she was, a pukka dean's daughter, tweeded up to the eyebrows, and she hadn't recognised a genuine peer of the realm when she saw one. But then I realised that my sympathy was misconceived and, if expressed, would have been simply an impertinence, for she behaved exactly as if the previous exchanges with his lordship had never occurred.

'I am extremely glad to meet you, Lord Brattling,' she said, shaking his hand. 'What a beautiful house you have! I am afraid that this is a part of the county with which I am not too familiar. I live at East Widdlethorpe; the Dower House, you know. Well, we must take up no more of your valuable time than is necessary. This, by the way,' she went on, indicating the humble representative of the lower classes at her side, 'is Oh-bwah, our tutor. Oh-bwah, I think you had better get the students together, and then perhaps Lord Brattling will be ready to take us to see his monuments.'

'Yes, do that, old chap,' said his lordship, lifting me out of the peasant class. 'Then we'll stroll over and have a look at the barrows. Oh, by the way, I'd like to have a word with you before you finally leave.'

The task of rounding up the herd was sufficiently onerous to give me no time to wonder what he meant by this last statement. They'd wandered all over the place, and I had the devil of a job to get them all together again. In fact, when we finally shambled off in the wake of Lord Brattling and Mrs Gorlestone there were still some missing. Katherine and Saham, for instance, weren't there. This was depressing, although I tried to argue that they were, after all, engaged, and it was therefore not surprising that they should prefer their own company to that of the mouldering Struldbrugs. I couldn't see Iris, either.

Lord Brattling was waiting for us at the entrance to an extensive wood.

'Well, it's a bit overgrown in parts,' he said, addressing the mob. 'Some of you may find it a little difficult. But the barrows are well worth seeing, if you get that far. Right. Follow me.'

He strode off into the wood, swinging a sort of young scythe on a long straight handle. The rest of us followed, doubtfully. As he said, the wood was a bit overgrown. We skirted several thickets, but at length we came to one that simply had to be penetrated, for the best of the barrows lay in its midst. A knee-high net of brambles lay across the way, and the only thornless space was occupied by a small, well-concealed bog. His lordship did his best to clear a path with his hook, but it would have taken ten Lord Brattlings to make much impression. Not that it would have been advisable to have ten of them on the go at once. One was enough. I suppose he was used to strolling about on his own, with a casual slash here and a careless swish there. After the first few steps into the thicket I thought it best to drop well behind him.

Thorn and bog took their inevitable toll of the company, and it was a mere dozen intrepid spirits that achieved the summit of the barrow. There we sank down to examine our wounds and listen to Lord Brattling on Celtic monuments. In spite of Peter's confident assertion I expected a load of old railway sleepers from his lordship, but in fact what he said was succinct, comprehensible, and, as far as I could judge, full of good reasoning. What with the soft, mossy turf, the discrete frettings of assorted wildfowl, his lordship's gentle rumble, and the complete absence of Mrs Gorlestone (last seen up to her fetlocks in slime and sinking fast) it was a pleasant ten minutes. However, it couldn't last. A beetle ran up my sleeve, some maniac took a distant pot at the rooks and pigeons, and Mrs Gorlestone burst through the bushes like a tweeded Diana.

'Mr Oh-bwah!' she trumpeted. 'The party is becoming scattered. May I suggest that you get them all together before you proceed.'

'Oh, I don't know,' I said. 'They can't very well get lost. And anyway we've got several barrows to see yet. I don't think we can wait for everyone to catch up.'

And with that I pressed after Lord Brattling, who had taken off at the first sight of Mrs Gorlestone and was already hacking a path through the jungle. In fact, I was so eager to escape that I forgot the elementary precaution of keeping a good two yards behind the scything peer, and only a swift sideways leap saved me from losing both legs to the follow-through of a particularly flamboyant swing. I'd hardly begun to tremble at the narrowness of the squeak when his lordship, neatly changing hands, caught me a glancing blow on the right shin. My involuntary oath made him turn round.

'What?' he enquired.

I said it again, indicating the reason for my discontent.

'Good God!' he said, gazing at the rip in my trouser-leg. 'Are you all right?'

'A mere scratch,' I said, bravely. 'Carry on.'

'I tell you what,' he said. 'Go back to the house, and get them to put a bandage round it. Don't worry about your people. I'll deal with them.'

I felt this was wise counsel. If only I'd kept the Wordsworth boots on with the other clobber instead of shedding them in Mardle, I'd have got off with nothing more than a nasty bruise, but already I could see red through the slit, and I wasn't prepared to bleed to death for the sake of a few lousy APES. So I legged it back to the house, and it wasn't long before I found myself at the main door. A few knocks produced nothing whatsoever, and in a state of desperation to which the wound, my exertions, and the overheating produced by two sets of clothing all contributed, I opened the door and entered. The hall was furnished with everything a good hall should contain except a welcoming flunkey, butler, or hostess. I coughed twice; the effect was like dropping a pebble into the Grand Canyon. Then I said 'Hello' several times. This was, if anything, worse. There was a fire alarm behind the door, but rather than resort to extreme measures I moved through the hall, hoping to find a few servants' quarters, a butler's pantry, or at least a tap, for my head was beginning to buzz. The first door I opened revealed a set of stairs leading downwards into darkness, the second a set of stairs leading upwards into a blank wall. The third took me into what was no doubt the Green Saloon, but which to me was simply the Revolving Room. I teetered aimlessly into the middle of a vast desert of grey Wilton, and passed out.

I opened my eyes to find the backside of an Old English sheepdog bending over me. After the first shudder had subsided, however, I saw it was only Tony Saham, with his face averted.

'There's damn all wrong with him that I can see,' he said, speaking to some third party. 'Nothing that a jug of water won't cure.'

'He looks pretty ghastly to me,' said another voice. Its pleasant tones and a glimpse of honey-coloured hair enabled me to identify this *tertium quid* as Katherine Southwood.

'He looks pretty ghastly most of the time,' said Saham. 'Anyway, I'm damned if I'm going to give him the kiss of life.'

I was with him there.

'All right, then,' said the girl. 'If you won't, I will.'

I shut my eyes with a snap.

'Like hell you will,' growled Saham.

'That's right, like hell I will,' she said. 'Now then, lift up his shoulders a little. Oh, come *on,* Tony!'

Saham put his hands under my shoulders and lifted, using, I thought, unnecessary force. I let my head fall back a little.

'That's funny,' she said. 'His mouth ought to open.'

I parted my lips.

'Delayed action,' she said.

The next moment Saham's fingers fastened in a vice-like grip on my nose, causing me to emit a snort that hit the ceiling like the last trump.

'Ah!' he shouted, letting me go with a bump. 'I told you there was nothing wrong with him.'

I opened my eyes again. This time the prospect was far more pleasing, for the girl's face was only inches away.

'Well,' I murmured, 'aren't you going to finish off the treatment?'

For a moment she hesitated; then she rose, and said coolly:

'What are you doing here?'

'That,' I said, 'is a good question. I suppose I must have passed out. The heat, you know. And, of course, my leg.'

'What's wrong with your leg?' asked Saham, sceptically.

'Take a look.'

'One, two,' he said, plonkingly. 'They're all there.'

'Take a closer look.'

To help them I gave the wounded member a slight flourish. The girl gave a cry. So did I.

'Hell's bells,' I added. 'Look at the carpet.'

The wilton now had a saucer-size bloodstain among its faded roses.

'How did you do it?' asked the girl.

'His lordship tried to hew it off,' I said. 'Fortunately 'twas but a glancing blow, and I'll be able to walk again in a couple of months or so.'

'Silly ass,' she said. 'I thought he'd get someone with that hook. Well, we ought to stanch the flow, I suppose. Can't let you bleed to death, especially on the best carpet. Do you think you could stagger over to the sofa? Right. Now, stay there. I'll go and find some water and a bandage, or something. Tony, come and help.'

She went out. Saham, looking about as pleasant as a yak with ulcers, followed. I relaxed among the cushions, wondering how I was going to explain all this to his lordship.

Presently Katherine returned, alone, bearing a bowl, a towel, and a roll of bandage.

'Who did you see?' I asked.

'Who? Oh, no-one,' she said, putting the things down on the floor by my feet. 'Right. Take your trousers off.'

'What!' I said, shocked. 'Here?'

'You've got pants on, presumably?'

'Well, yes,' I admitted. 'But I don't think this is the place - and in front of you -'

'Oh, don't worry about me,' she said. 'I shall probably shriek and fall down in a swoon, but that'll be all. Anyway, I can't do anything unless I can see the wound properly.'

I stood up, and turning my back modestly on her, dropped the trouserings. I had forgotten for the moment that they were but the outer shell.

'I'm sorry,' she said, when she felt able to speak. 'I hadn't expected anything as sensational as that. An old half-witted sheep in wolf's clothing, so to speak. Do you know, I *thought* there was something familiar about Morley Swanton's voice. Well, I'm afraid you'll have to slip the breeches off as well. Golly! You can see why they're called a pair. Right, let's have a look at your leg.'

'How is it?' I asked, sinking back into the massive sofa.

'Bloody but unbowed. I don't think we'll have to whip it off, anyway.'

'Good. Tell me,' I went on, airing a subject that was worrying me, 'how did you happen to find me in here? I mean, I knew you and your - well, Tony - had wandered off somewhere, but I assumed it would be to some secluded spot.'

'We did. As a matter of fact, I wanted to get rid of my encumbrance.'

'Saham?'

'The stomacher.'

'But I thought you took it off at Mardle?'

'Well, it suddenly struck me that old Sherlock Gorlestone might have another sneak round our rooms while we were at the lecture. So I put it on again. Just as well, for she gave my room another going-over.'

'Ah!' I said. 'Yes, I remember she went out before the lecture began. That was bright of you.'

'I'm not so sure about that. You've no idea what it's like lugging the best part of Moby Dick around with you, especially on a hot day. Anyway, I thought I'd take it off. As a matter of fact, I haven't had time to do it yet, what with Tony and corpses on the carpet and so on. Now, keep still while I bandage you. There,' she said, tying the last knot, 'that'll do for the time being. Now I think I'll climb out of this corset, before I'm crippled for life. You can put your trousers on again. Don't bother about the breeches. We'll dispose of them somewhere.'

She walked over to a folding screen in the corner of the room and disappeared behind it. Marvelling at her sang-froid in a strange house, I heaved myself up. The remnants of the breeches caught my eye. It wouldn't do to leave them visible for one second longer than was necessary, so I shoved them under a cushion. I had just got one foot into the trousers when a slight noise made me turn like a faun surpriz'd. On the terrace outside the French windows stood Mrs Gorlestone.

'Woof!' called the girl from behind the screen. 'Free at last! For this relief, much thanks. Here, catch!'

And like the great devil fish, *manta birostris,* leaping from the tropical ocean, the corset soared into the air.

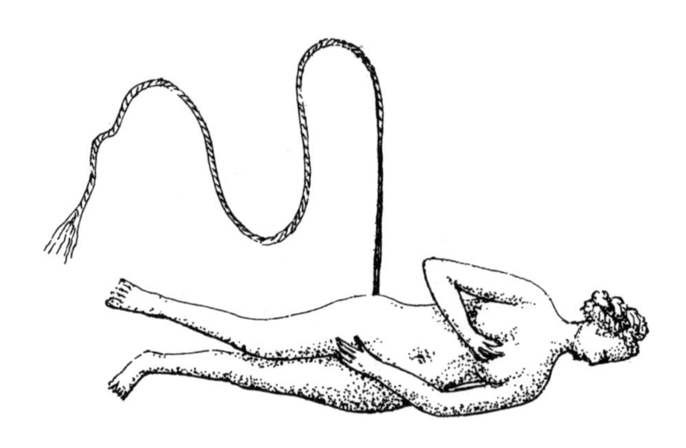

12

'Mr Oh-bwah!' said Mrs Gorlestone, advancing. 'Cover your limbs!'

On the word 'limbs', the corset touched down in the midst of an elaborate cut-glass-and-wrought-iron chandelier. For a moment it seemed that it was going straight through, for it folded and slipped; then some loop or snag caught on a spike, and it hung there, leaving about six inches of silk and whalebone drooping beneath the lowest branch.

'I heard a gel's voice,' said Mrs Gorlestone.

I stared. I'd expected her to leap upon the Lost Article with a glad cry and press it to her bosom, although, in practical terms, this would have involved a vertical spring of eight feet or so. Then it dawned upon me that, turned half away from that end of the room and having her eye, moreover, bent upon my indecent legs, she hadn't observed the flight of the corset.

'Mr Oh-bwah, I heard a gel's voice,' she repeated.

'A parlourmaid?'

'Don't trifle with me, Mr Oh-bwah. I distinctly heard a gel's voice. Aha!'

She spotted the screen and galloped over to it, passing directly underneath her corset. Handicapped as I was by having only one trousered leg, I could do nothing to stop her. With an imperious gesture she twitched the screen aside. It swayed and fell, revealing Katherine in the act of zipping up her dress.

'Miss Southwood!' snorted Mrs Gorlestone. 'I thought so.'

'Hello, Mrs Gorlestone,' said the girl, calmly completing the zip.

'Why are you behind this screen?'

'Well, I couldn't take my dress off in front of Mr Hautbois.'

'And why, may I ask, was it necessary to take off your dress?'

'A small discomfort. A twisted strap, or something.'

'Really,' said Mrs Gorlestone, 'do you expect me to believe that? I find Mr Oh-bwah - Mr Oh-bwah! I had expected you to be properly clad by this time. Please adjust your clothes - I find Mr Oh-bwah in an indecent state, and you, gel, behind a screen, obviously in the act of getting dressed or undressed, and you expect me to believe that the two are unconnected? And in Lord Brattling's house! Really, words fail me.'

As a matter of fact, they came out like a Texan gusher. Our feeble attempts to stop the flow were simply knocked aside, and the presence of a small but interested crowd of APES seemed merely to encourage her to greater and greater innuendo. Even when, decently trousered, I pointed to the bloodstain in the carpet, she refused to believe in the severity of the wound; indeed, she seemed to think that a laboratory test would prove that it wasn't even my blood. In desperation I called on Saham, who had just come in, to confirm that I'd been lying there when they found me. This he did, reluctantly.

'And what was Mr Oh-bwah's state?' demanded Mrs Gorlestone.

'Well,' said Saham, slowly, 'he seemed to have passed out. But he woke up the moment Kay - Miss Southwood - began to give him the kiss of life.'

'Ah! She kissed you?' said Mrs Gorlestone, turning to me.

'Unfortunately we never actually made contact. And anyway, it was purely medicinal.'

'And what happened then?' she asked, going back to Saham.

'Oh, he got on to the sofa.'

'By himself?'

'Well, nobody helped him.'

'Did he appear to be badly injured?' continued the attorney-general.

'No.'

'Do you think it was necessary for him to remove his trousers?'

'No, not to have the cut dressed.'

'Louse,' I said.

'When did he remove his trousers?' asked Mrs Gorlestone, ignoring me.

'I don't know. I wasn't here when he did it. I went out of the room with Kay to get some water and bandage. I didn't come back with her.'

'Why not, Mr Saham?'

'That's my business,' he said, sullenly.

She gave him a pretty austere look, and I could see that she was on the point of asking herself if she could treat him as a hostile witness. But at that moment Dr Bawdeswell nosed forward.

'Excuse me,' he said, 'I - er - happened to be passing the window when Mr Hautbois removed his trousers. I saw that Miss Southwood was with him.'

'And what,' said Mrs Gorlestone, 'did they do after he removed his trousers?'

'I fear I was not able to see,' said Dr Bawdeswell. 'Mr Hautbois sank down into the sofa, and Miss Southwood also disappeared behind it. They were there for quite ten minutes.'

'Oh, hell's bells,' I said. 'It didn't take that long. Five, at the most.'

'And then?' asked Mrs Gorlestone, still ignoring me.

'Then Miss Southwood got up and walked away,' said the doctor. 'She seemed - but I must stress that I could not see very well - she seemed to be adjusting her dress.'

'May I say a few words?' said Lord Brattling, pushing his way through the crowd. 'After all, if a crime has been committed, it's been committed in my house.'

Mrs Gorlestone, suddenly reminded that she wasn't on her own midden, began to apologise for the disturbance that two thoughtless young people had caused. And not only thoughtless but, she was afraid, immodest. Mr Oh-bwah would, of course, pay for the carpet. As there seemed to be upwards of one-third of an acre of it I waited with interest to see if he would accept this offer.

'Oh, come, *de minimis non curat lex,'* he said. There was a small murmur of appreciation from the crowd. This was the sort of language one expected from a peer. 'Anyway, what's a bloody spot among friends?' he went on. 'And it was entirely my fault that Mr Hautbois was injured. Now, this other matter. Mr Hautbois, you say you were out cold on the carpet, until you were revived by the kiss of life?'

'Well,' I said, 'to be quite accurate, I came round before she actually kissed me.'

'The threat was enough, eh? Well, never mind. You then retired to the sofa and had your leg bandaged, having first removed your trousers. Would you have removed them if you'd known that Mr. Saham was not going to return to the room?'

'If you don't mind me saying so,' I said, 'that's a funny way to put it. As a matter of fact, I don't give a cusser's tink what Mr Saham does. And anyway, I didn't take them off until Miss Southwood got back. She told me to. She said she couldn't get at the cut unless I did.'

He nodded. 'Reasonable. It was a pretty sharp nick, and dammit, you've got enough bandage on your leg to put an elephant's arse in a sling. Now, the question is, did she limit her comfort to bandaging, or was there a spot of dalliance on the side?'

'Certainly not!'

'H'm. Not tactful to sound quite so revolted, old chap. Girls are sensitive about that sort of thing. Well, now we come to the evidence of Dr Bawdy. He swears he saw the female accused walking away from the sofa and displaying some sweet disorder in the dress. What exactly she was doing, zipping or unzipping, buttoning or unbuttoning, is not clear. No doubt the doctor averted his gaze. Well, what do you say to that?' he asked, turning to Katherine.

She shrugged. 'It must have been a trick of his imagination,' she said. 'I didn't start to unzip until I was behind the screen.'

'And why,' he inquired, gently, 'did you have to unzip at all?'

'Something was digging me in the ribs.'

'Mr Hautbois's finger?'

'Not unless he'd detached it from his hand. No, it was part of my underwear. I couldn't adjust it without slipping off my dress.'

'So your sole reason for going behind the screen was to avoid embarrassing Mr Hautbois?'

'Very nicely put,' said the girl.

'Are you comfortable now?'

'Very,' she said. And she seemed to be.

'Well,' he said, turning back to Mrs Gorlestone, 'I think that's cleared it all up.'

'Pardon me, Lord Brattling,' she said, 'but I am afraid I cannot agree with you. What you could not know, of course, is that this incident is merely the latest in a whole series of improprieties between these two irresponsible young people. For example, they contrived to be left behind on our visit to Swinesthorpe Castle, and arrived back at Great Mardle extremely late and with some ridiculous story about an owl and a bicycle.'

'Indeed!' said Lord Brattling. 'An owl and a bicycle?'

'A *stuffed* owl.'

'Of course.'

'And on Tuesday Miss Southwood was seen - again by Dr. Bawdeswell - to come from Mr Oh-bwah's bedroom. There has, I fear, been a great deal of impropriety.'

'Dear, dear,' said his lordship. He turned to the girl. '*Have* you been improper with Mr Hautbois?'

'No.'

'What, never?'

'No, never.'

'Good enough,' he said. 'Mrs Gorlestone, your suspicions are groundless.'

'I fear,' she said, drawing herself up, 'that a mere denial carries little weight with me. My acquaintance with Miss Southwood, though short, has been rather longer than yours, Lord Brattling, and I think I am therefore better qualified to judge her character. Moreover, as President-elect of the APES and hostess of this Summer School, I have a responsibility for her moral well-being that you cannot pretend to.'

'Oh, I don't know,' he said, mildly. 'After all, I *am* her father.'

There was a stunned silence at this. Even Mrs Gorlestone was speechless.

'Or so her mother tells me,' he went on. He looked at his watch. 'By the way, my wife has got tea for you all in the kitchen. It ought to be ready now. If you'd like to follow Kate, she'll lead you to it. Kate, save a cup for Mr Hautbois. I want him to have a squint at my mushroom houses first. This way, Hautbois.'

As I followed him to the french window my dazed eye happened to catch the corset. Something had disturbed it, and it now hung from a single hook, almost clear of the crystal drops. The APES, thirsting for tea, were already trooping out of the door at the other end of the room, but I couldn't take any chances. I nipped smartly back and twitched the thing clear. Clutching it to my heart, I sidled to the window and in a moment was out in the good fresh air. Lord Brattling was waiting for me.

'Ah,' he said, watching me with interest as I stuffed it carefully up my jersey, 'so that's what Kate had to get rid of. Must have been damned uncomfortable.'

'It's a long story -' I began.

'Oh, well, I expect Kate will give me the gist of it sooner or later. Now, come and tell me what you think of my mushrooms.'

Three-quarters of an hour later, after an extremely interesting discussion of spawning, sterilisation, peak heat, damping off, Bacterial Blotch, and Mummy Disease, I climbed into the coach and started counting heads.

'All here?' asked the driver, starting his engine.

'Two short.'

He muttered something coarse and stopped it.

'Does anyone,' I asked, 'know what has happened to Mr Gorlestone and Miss Overy?'

No-one did, and the look on Mrs Gorlestone's face was enough to prevent any theories being aired. We settled down to wait. Katherine and Saham were sitting together on the front seat, but the conversation didn't seem to be exactly flowing. The rest of the crowd, however, chattered away, discussing, if the snatches I heard were typical, the pros and cons of living in a stately home. After about ten minutes I was beginning to think of organising a search party, but before I could do anything Patty Colkirk's voice rose high above the general matter to announce that she had sighted the truants. I got out of the coach and went a few steps to meet them.

'Oh, hello, William,' said Iris. 'Are we dreadfully late?'

She looked tired, and a little fed-up.

'Had a nice time?' I asked, as they got into the coach.

'Oh, absolutely *lovely,'* she said, in her most penetrating tones. 'Mr Gorlestone has been teaching me the Scouts' Way.'

I shot a glance at Mr Gorlestone. He'd evidently just seen the look on his mother's face. I took pity on him.

'Sit next to Miss Colkirk,' I whispered.

He obeyed. Iris, following my gesture, took the seat behind the driver. I made my way up the coach and sat down next to Mrs Gorlestone.

'Home, James,' I called.

At least I wouldn't have to talk for the next half-hour.

Supper continued the rest-cure that the Quiet Half-Hour in the coach had begun. I was wedged between Hester Catton and the Human Gannet, and neither of these made any great demands. The lecture, too, was relaxing - Tom Didlington on the Borshire dialect. Masterly. As I climbed the stairs after seeing him off I felt that things could have been worse. True, my leg was aching, Katherine was engaged to a bearded louse, and I'd lost my chance of a permanent place on Mrs Gorlestone's christmas-card list; but on the other hand I was still more or less alive, I was on cordial terms with a fungiphile peer, I'd had a very entertaining evening, and tea was brewing in the kitchen.

'Coffee, Mr Hautbois?' asked Patty Colkirk, brandishing a pot and slopping a few fluid ounces on to the floor.

'Well,' I said, 'if there's any tea I think I'd prefer that.'

'Plenty,' she said, catching up another pot and filling a cup and saucer for me. 'Oh, sorry. Mr Gorlestone, another cup?'

I retired to the wall and took stock of the company. Patty Colkirk, pressing another cup to Dick Gorlestone's manly bosom. Queenie Winch, Elsie Cockthorpe, and Stan Hoe brewing their own poison and discussing, astoundingly, the *Rime of the Ancient Mariner*. Dr Bawdeswell, Cyril Thrigby, Roger, and Saham at the sink end with Iris and Katherine. Quite a crowd, in a room fifteen by eight.

'Ah, the wounded hero,' said Roger, spying me. 'You look pale and interesting, Bill. Come and tell me the sober truth about this astonishing happening at Brattling Hall. I can get naught but whispers of bloody strife and deeds of shame from this lot.'

'Oh, it was nothing much,' I said, joining them. 'Lord Brattling took a slice off my leg, so I had to have it bound up. And there was some misunderstanding about the circumstances.'

'Was that all? I heard a rumour that you'd been caught in fragrant delight with some woman.'

'No such luck,' I said. 'Anyway, it's a bit of a delicate subject, so be a good chap and belt up.'

'No-one,' said Roger, 'is more skilled at the subtle hint than you are. Right, I'll change the subject. I've had a thrilling day, if anyone's interested. Keats in the afternoon, Coleridge at night. Not in person, of course.'

'And who,' asked Dr Bawdeswell, 'did you manage to capture to read the Ancient Mariner to your students? I gather it was something of a coup to get Morley Swanton.'

'Oh, I was just lucky,' said Roger, modestly. 'Only a slight acquaintance. I hear your visiting lecturer this morning was a sensation?'

'He was marvellous,' said Iris. 'An absolute darling. So virile. Don't you think so, Katherine dear?'

'Well, he was a bit whiskery for my taste.'

'Oh, I wasn't thinking of his whiskers,' said Iris. 'Anyway, dear, I thought you were rather partial to a whisker or two?'

'You could hardly call Humphrey Godwick's ornaments a whisker or two,' I said. 'And he's pretty ancient, underneath it all. Well over the Aristotlian optimum. Too old for either of you.'

'Certainly too old for *me,'* said Katherine.

'Oh, but I thought you preferred the mature man?' said Iris, sweetly. 'Weren't you rather taken with Morley Swanton? He looked at least ninety. Although I must admit that those breeches of his were rather fetching. And do you know, it's very odd, but there was something frightfully familiar about his legs. I felt sure that I'd seen them before somewhere, but of course I suppose I haven't.'

'Perhaps,' said Katherine, 'you were lovers in a previous existence.'

'Well,' I said, cutting in, for I felt that all this joshing was taking us on to dangerous ground, 'I'm afraid tomorrow may seem a little flat after all these alarms and excursions. The excursion'll be there, but no alarms, I hope. A few churches and a wander round Borwich. And the evening's free.'

'Come, come, old boy,' said Roger. 'Aren't you forgetting the social?'

'The what?'

'The social. The high spot of the week. Historic Borshire and Romantic Literature have been simply a front to cover secret preparations for the social. They've been going on for days. There's even a list of performers. I've put you down to sing "The Stately Homes of England" and "I'll take you home again, Katherine".'

'Kathleen, you mean.'

'Oh, do I? Anyway, Iris is going to give her all as the Serpent of Old Nile -'

'Can I choose my own Antony?' asked Iris.

'Certainly. Give me the name in a sealed envelope. Katherine here will lead us in "Knees up, Mother Brown" and organise the egg-and-spoon race, and young Saham will oblige with his rendering of the Green-Eyed Monster - sorry, I mean "The Green Eye of the Little Yellow God". All continuous and obligatory entertainment. No sneaking off for a quiet snog in the moonlight.'

'With who?' I asked, ungrammatically.

'Oh, I thought you might have someone lined up. We'll have to see what we can do for you. Barton-Bendish Computer Dating Service. Now, let's have a few details. What would you like? Blonde or brunette?'

'Well, neither, really.'

'Bald, eh? Kinky.'

'No, what I mean is, something between blonde and brunette.'

'About the shade of young Southwood here? Just as a guide.'

'Oh, I didn't know you were a guide too, Miss Southwood,' said Dick Gorlestone, joining us. 'Miss Colkirk is Tawny Owl. She's just been telling me about the wonderful things they do on the South Downs.'

'Oh, God!' said Saham. 'Excuse me.' And he pushed his way out of the room.

'The merest whiff of Baden-Powell gets him going,' said Roger.

'You seem to have got it in for him,' I said, speaking low.

'No, no,' said Roger, also sotto. He eased me away a little. 'Just friendly joshing. Plus, of course, the fact that he's a rival for the job. All's fair - if he gets narky he might just speak the odd word out of turn to old Subcourse or Mrs G. He's certainly pretty strong with them at the moment, so anything I can do to wobble his perch will be a help. And I was a bit miffed that he left me in the lurch and joined your lot today. I suppose he couldn't trust his popsie to resist your fatal charm. She left me, too.'

'A nasty knock to your ratings. But are you serious about this mouldy social?'

'Well, there's certainly some sort of rave happening. Ask Mr Gorlestone.'

Dick Gorlestone confirmed that there was to be a camp-fire sing-song on the last night of the School. For his sins, he'd got the job of arranging the entertainment, and he was hoping that one of the younger people would lend a hand. How about Mr Barton-Bendish?

'Good God, no,' said Roger. 'I'm hopeless at party games. There must be someone else. What about Miss Overy? She knows some fascinating games.'

'You say the nicest things,' said Iris.

'Would you really help?' asked Mr Gorlestone, eagerly. 'Miss Colkirk has agreed to lend a hand, but I think we need some ideas from the younger generation.'

This was bit unfair on Miss Colkirk, who, if not exactly in the first flush of youth, was a babe-in-arms compared with the majority of the APES. I was surprised that he even dared to come within barge-pole length of Iris, after the dressing-down he'd had when we'd got back from Brattling. It had been audible the length of the corridor. He must be pretty deeply smitten to defy his mother. Iris, I noticed, was looking a bit dubious about it, but eventually she agreed to help and they went off with Patty Colkirk for a little get-together downstairs in the lounge. The others also began to drift away, and presently only Roger, Dr Bawdeswell, Katherine, and myself were left in the kitchen.

'May I give you a hand?' asked Dr Bawdeswell, seeing the girl move towards the sink.

'No, thank you,' she said, coolly. 'There's hardly anything here.'

'Nonsense,' he said, sidling up. 'We really can't allow you to do it all by yourself. At least let me dry the cups.'

'Let young Hautbois do it,' said Roger. 'It'll be good practice for him. Anyway, I know why you're so keen to help, Joseph, you lecherous old goat. I haven't noticed you springing to the sink when Edith's there. You wait till she hears about this!'

Dr Bawdeswell seemed to go pale.

'You wouldn't tell her -' he began.

'I jolly well would. She'll have you chained to the washing-up bowl for months on end. Unless, of course, you go quietly now.'

The doctor went, quietly.

'H'm,' I said. 'Blackmail. Who's Edith?'

'My aunt,' said Roger. 'Married old Joseph there by brute force in 1938. He leads a dog's life. Type-cast for the part. I have to crack the whip now and then, especially when there's any crump- er, girls around, or he'd be up in court twice a month.'

'Talking of girls,' I said, idly, 'where's your fancy tonight? Sandra, isn't it?'

'Oh, here and there,' said Roger. His manner struck me as a trifle embarrassed. 'Er - excuse me, Katherine, I must have a word in Bill's ear.'

He drew me to the door.

'We've parted,' he murmured. 'Mutually. To be frank, old chap, and this is just between the two of us, she's a bit on the clinging side. And she's got practically no conversation.'

'What!' I said, amazed. 'That worries *you?*'

'Ssshh. In the circumstances, yes. She started hinting at engagement rings, and I suddenly found that I didn't want to be bound for life to a girl who has six ounces of kapok instead of the usual grey matter. So we parted, and she went off in a huff.'

'Lucky to get one at this time of night,' I said. 'Ah, well, that's life.'

'Yes. Well, I suppose I might as well have an early night,' he said, mournfully. 'See you tomorrow, I suppose.'

'Thanks for this morning's performance.'

'Ah. Any time,' he said, and sloped off.

'The tumult and the shouting dies,' I remarked, going back to the draining board and picking up a teaspoon. 'The captains and the kings depart. I suppose it's too much to hope that you've got an humble and a contrite heart?'

'Me?' said Katherine. 'What have I got to be contrite about?'

'Keeping your social status dark. It confused us all. Mrs Gorlestone was most upset.'

'I know,' she said, smiling. 'Do you know why?'

'Well, she'd just been giving you a tremendous roasting, and then she found your father -'

'Yes, but that's not all. I only found this out today. Apparently someone told her that the girls had been saying that one of the Borwich High mistresses was the daughter of a peer, and from something that I'd said, quite innocently, about my father growing mushrooms, she deduced it must be Iris. And so she set poor Richard on to improve himself by a good marriage.'

'Good lord! How do you know this?'

'Well, my room's next to hers, and when they had a few words before supper I couldn't help hearing. Anyway, Richard still hankers after Iris, but of course he won't get a look-in there, will he?'

'How should I know?'

'Well, I thought you might. And anyway, I fancy that Miss Colkirk has got her eye on him now. I bet he'll be sharing her tent at camp next Easter.'

'Well, you see what comes of not revealing your origins,' I said. 'Lives ruined all over the place. Even I had no idea - but now I look at you,' I went on, stepping back to admire her, 'I can see you're the daughter of a hundred earls.'

'That,' she said, 'is a gross slander on my mother. Anyway, father's only a baron.'

'Of course,' I said. 'It all comes back to me now. Southwood - the family name. And if he'd been an earl, you'd have been a lady.'

'I'm not sure that I like that way of putting it. But you're right. As it is, as a younger daughter I'm not even an honourable.'

'Bad luck. Still, you *are* a minor member of the peerage.'

She stared out of the window into the darkness. 'Does it make any difference?' she said.

'Well -' I began, taking up a wet cup with a hand that trembled slightly.

'Mr Oh-bwah!'

The cup flew in the air. I dived instinctively, and caught it on the first bounce. Plastic.

'Mr Oh-bwah,' said Mrs Gorlestone, in the doorway, 'have you seen Mr Gorlestone recently?'

I got slowly up from the floor. After all she's said about me today, I thought, she's got a ruddy crust to come wandering in here with a casual enquiry about her mouldy son. On the other hand, she must have thought I'd got a ruddy crust to go and sit next to her in the coach. Perhaps she took that as the first tentative step in a *rapprochement?* And anyway, I was willing to let bygones be bygones, within reason. So I answered temperately that I thought he was down in the lounge, planning the social.

'Thank you,' she said, sitting down on the only chair in the room. 'Mr Oh-bwah, I should be obliged if you would tell Mr Gorlestone that I wish to see him. I shall wait here.'

This was an unwelcome interruption to my conversation with Katherine, but short of starting another rough-house I had no alternative but to do as the old autocrat wished. And worse was to follow. As I ascended the stairs with Dick Gorlestone at my heels, I met Katherine and Saham, descending.

'Off somewhere?' I asked.

'Just going for a stroll in the park to take advantage of the moonlight,' said Saham, smirking. 'Any objections?'

I looked at Katherine, but she seemed to be quite content with the arrangement.

'No, not really,' I said, gloomily.

'Good,' he said.

They passed down the stairs. I dropped Dick at the kitchen door and went to my room, pondering on the slings and arrows. For a moment during my recent conversation with Katherine I'd thought we might be on the verge of something delicate; but then Mrs Gorlestone had barged in, and now Katherine was going off, perfectly happy, for an amorous stroll with Saham. No doubt I'd been quite mistaken about that moment at the sink. And although she'd been quite friendly during the day, and had, of course, helped me tremendously over the affair with the corset, there wasn't a shred of evidence that this was anything more than a product of her general good-will and sympathy for the underdog; in other words, she cared no more for me than for, say, the poor man at the gate, and a great deal less for either of us than for Saham. After all, she *was* engaged to him, and she must, therefore, feel something out of the ordinary for him. The engagement was solid fact. And solid facts are what we historians have to work on; hopes are no bloody use at all.

I toileted morosely, and had just climbed into my pyjamas when there was a tap at the door.

'Come in,' I called. Roger, no doubt, in another muddle.

In fact, it was Iris. In a dressing-gown.

'Oh, William dear,' she said. 'May I come in?'

'Yes, of course. Excuse my déshabille.'

She came in and closed the door behind her. 'Are you sure? I mean, I don't want to get you into any more trouble.'

'I like having you here. You brighten up an old man's life.'

She sank down on to the bed. 'Oh, don't put yourself among the old men, William dear. I don't think I could bear it.'

I took the basket chair. 'Had a hard day?'

'Frightful. Especially this afternoon. How to make a camp-fire in three easy lessons. He fixed me with his glittering eye.'

'I bet he did. You'd make anyone's eye glitter,' I said, hoping to cheer her up. 'Pity you missed all the fun at the house, though.'

'Yes, but Katherine told me all about it. Too funny for words, darling. By the way, I may be able to help you to return Mrs Gorlestone's armour-plate. It'll be rather public, so I won't give you any details, in case anything goes wrong.'

'Iris,' I said, gratefully, 'you're an angel.'

'Am I really? But the trouble with angels, William dear, is that they're more or less untouchable, aren't they?'

'Not when they come down to earth,' I said, getting up and sitting, rather heavily, beside her on the bed.

'Darling, you've had a wearing day. Perhaps I'd better go. I'm keeping you from your bed.'

'Well, hardly that,' I said, putting a tentative arm round her. 'I was simply going to bed for a quiet read, to soothe the jangled nerves.'

She leant across and picked up my bedside book. '*Barchester Towers.* How nice. To bed with a soothing Trollope.' She put the book down, and lay back on the pillow. 'Darling, won't I do instead?'

I had the feeling that we'd been here before, only on the previous occasion I hadn't known that Katherine was engaged to Saham, and now I did. Should it make any difference? Must I cling to the memory of Rothschild's grackles, or should I take the cash in hand and waive the rest?

Iris raised herself on one elbow. The dressing-gown slipped away from her shoulder, revealing that her nightdress didn't amount to anything much.

'This,' I murmured, 'is almost more than flesh and blood can stand.'

'What an anatomical way of putting things. What's the matter, William?

You don't seem very happy.' And she leant forward and began to nuzzle my shoulder.

'Well...oh, dammit, sorry. It's not your fault,' I said.

'Can I help?' Her voice was indistinct. She seemed to be trying to unbutton my pyjama jacket with her teeth.

'Well, you might.'

'Rather grudging, William darling. If you don't look out I shall have to look for someone else to comfort me,' she said, running a warm hand down my spine from nape to coccyx.

'Well, there's always Scout Gorlestone,' I said, responding, rather unimaginatively, with a similar gesture, 'or Roger.'

'Roger?' she murmured, beginning to explore, 'I expect he's snug in bed with Sandra Litcham.'

'Oh, no. At least I shouldn't think so. He told me they'd parted.'

She jerked her head up sharply, causing me to bite the end of my tongue.

'Strewth!' I said, with a tear starting to my eye.

'Sorry, darling. What did you say about Roger?'

'Parted from Sandra. Fighting terms. She started to babble of rings and things, so he quit while still in the black.'

'Well, well, well.' She sank back on to the pillow and lay there, deep in thought. Courteously respecting her evident desire for seclusion, I moved slightly away, a bit relieved, to be honest, that the clinch had been broken. The movement brought her back to the present.

'Darling! I'm sorry. A passing thought, that's all.'

'So I saw. Roger?'

She nodded.

'Ah,' I said. 'Well, that's that, I suppose.' I got up from the bed.

'No, don't go yet, William darling,' she said. She seemed to have forgotten that we were in my room. 'Let me give you a teeny little thank-you kiss. Just for luck.'

'Well, if you put it like that, why not? And *honi soit qui mal y pense.'*

She stood up and put her arms round my neck. If the kiss that followed was a teeny little one, the large economy size would have taken us through to the small hours.

'So that's how it is!' said Tony Saham, flinging open the door and pensing mal like the dickens. 'I knew you were up to something. Right. *Right.* That's it. Wait till Kay hears about this!'

And he stalked away, leaving us clutching each other like a couple of drowning straws.

13

Thursday morning was wet. As we were due to tear round a few churches in a waterproof coach the weather was not of prime importance for Historic Borshire, but it had a generally depressive effect. At breakfast conversation was subdued, appetites small. I fielded one sharp, enigmatic glance from Katherine that told me nothing, but as she and Saham left the table together I knew it was only a matter of time before she would be in possession of his full, technicolor version of last night's discovery. My not inconsiderable gloom deepened. I was losing all along the line. I must already have blown my chances of getting the job of Resident Officer, I was on the point of losing the chance, admittedly faint, of detaching Katherine from Tony Saham, and the only girl who had shown herself to be unreservedly attracted to me was in love with my best friend.

The day continued to be gloomy. Iris didn't turn up at the coach, but sent a message to say that she'd decided to go to Mr Barton-Bendish's lecture on Southey and hoped I'd understand. Katherine and Saham were also absent when the time of departure arrived, and although I held up the coach for ten minutes there was no sign of them and we had to go. Going through my notes on the churches and directing the driver did nothing to lighten the gloom. Fortunately all three churches were full of intrinsic interest, and I hoped my increasing glumness would go unremarked. Lunch at the Blue Kipper Café in Shannyham-on-Sea did little to restore the spirit, and while the APES were buying souvenirs for their loved ones and wasting their substance on the riotous fruit-machines of the promenade I slipped down to the deserted beach and took it out on the cowering North Sea, throwing stones at it for twenty minutes and hitting it every time.

In the afternoon, a further gawp at the Decorated and the Perpendicular was followed by a short shopping-trip stop to buy goodies for the beanfeast. When we arrived back at Great Mardle the Romantics were already wolfing their tea and cakes. I spotted Katherine and Saham seated together, but although this in itself was a little cheering, as I'd been afraid, for no logical reason, that Katherine might have left the school altogether, I couldn't get near her, as Mrs Gorlestone grabbed me by the short and curlies to tell me about the arrangements for the evening's shindig. From her manner I deduced that she'd temporarily buried the hatchet, but it was obvious that she'd got the spot well marked. Then Dick Gorlestone and Patty Colkirk joined us, and by the time I was able to disengage myself everyone else had vanished, presumably to dish themselves up for the greatest social event of the season.

I made my way, dispiritedly, up to my room. It took me ten minutes to wash and change, so I was left with about an hour to spare before the start of the festivities. I lay down on the bed and took up my Trollope.

Some time later there was a knock on the door, and Roger breezed in.

'Wakey, wakey, rise and shine!' he said. 'Wake up, old lad.'

'What are you so ruddy cheerful about?' I asked, grumpily.

'What's up? Had a hard day?'

'Bloody.'

'Well, throw it all off and come and join in the merry-making.'

'Has it started?'

'Half an hour ago. Everyone's asking where you've got to.'

'Everyone?' I asked, hopefully.

'Well, Mrs G. She pinned me before I'd got in the door. I said I thought you'd be lounging in your pit, so she sent me to fie you out. I say, old chap, while we're alone, brace yourself for a piece of bad news.'

My heart hit the floor with a dull thud. 'What?' I asked.

'Well,' he said, slowly, 'I've just had a chat with Dr Subcourse, and he dropped a strong hint that he favoured me for the Residency.'

'Oh, *that?'* I said, relieved. 'Well, congratulations. Couldn't go to a better man.'

'You don't mind?'

'Not in the least. A week of this has been enough for me. I couldn't face making a career of it.'

'Well, old chap, this is hardly a typical week. And there've been compensations, surely?'

'Some.'

'By the way,' he said, off-handedly, 'what do you think of Iris?'

'She's a very nice girl.'

'You seem to get on pretty well with her?'

'We've had our moments,' I said, guardedly. 'But we're just good friends.'

'Ah. I'm afraid I pinched three of your lot today, by the way. Iris turned up for Southey, and then, blow me, if Saham and young Southwood didn't roll in. Said they'd missed the coach.'

'They didn't miss much else.'

'Cheer up, old boy. Come and mingle with the revellers. As a matter of fact, we'd better get down, or the greedy hogs will have scoffed all the grub.'

We wandered down. There was a supper-table laden with food just inside the door of the lounge, and we grabbed a plate apiece and helped ourselves to sausages on sticks, vol-au-vents, asparagus rolls, and what-nots. Then we turned to survey the company.

It was a scene of almost unimaginable splendour. Party frocks, many of them obvious heirlooms, were everywhere, and no fewer than four of the men - Dr Subcourse, Dr Bawdeswell, Dick Gorlestone, and Cyril Thrigby - were in dinner-jackets. On our side of the room the APES were buffeting with gay abandon. On the other side, Mrs Gorlestone was holding court in a silver-and-lace form-fitting dress that gave her a startling resemblance to the late Queen Mary - the woman, I mean, not the ship. At the bottom of the room a multi-coloured throng milled about another table which, from the number of people who came away bearing cups and glasses, I identified as the public drinking-trough. Sandra Litcham, the sixth-formers, and Tony Saham were in a little knot in another corner, but I couldn't see Iris or Katherine. Disappointed, I applied myself to the food.

'These vol-au-vents are good,' I said to Roger.

He didn't answer. I followed his gaze, and understood why he was pre-occupied. A swirl in the throng at the far end of the room had revealed Iris, serving cups of coffee. I suppose, if I'd been asked to guess what she would wear, I'd have plumped for something both snappy and revealing. I now saw how unsubtle that guess would have been. She was wearing a long, high-necked sari-type dress of some iridescent material that hid the boldness of her curves and made her look taller and slimmer than she really was - beating, in other words, Sandra Litcham on her own pitch. The effect was striking.

'Strewth!' I said. 'Look at that!'

Again Roger failed to answer. He put down his plate and moved off towards her like a man in a dream, still carrying a half-eaten sausage at the port. I followed, rather aimlessly, taking my plate for company, and nodding to an ancient or two on the way. When I was about fifteen feet from the table the crowd split again, and I stopped in my tracks.

Katherine was standing behind it, using a long ladle to fill the glasses of thirsty merrymakers. She was wearing a long, simple dress that was reminiscent of an early Georgian dairymaid's - oatmeal-coloured, lowish, rounded neckline, full skirt, and sleeves that stopped just below the elbow. She looked absolutely marvellous. I grabbed a glass and pushed my way through. She ladled me a half-pint of greenish fluid with a nice, easy action, keeping her head well down and her eye on the tumbler.

'What is it?' I asked, huskily.

'Mrs Gorlestone's lemonade,' she said, without looking up.

'It looks like nectar to me,' I said.

She didn't answer.

There were others to be served, so I retired to the side and found a seat that would give me a good view. I couldn't keep my eyes off her. It was most extraordinary. Some sort of homing device took charge of my head, and even if I managed, by a great effort of will, to look elsewhere, it was only a second or two before I found myself studying her again. Solid bodies, of course, intervened from time to time, and during one of these enforced interludes I noticed that Tony Saham was also watching her with some intensity. I toyed with the idea of heaving an asparagus roll at him, but I'd only got one left and, on balance, it didn't seem worth it.

At last the queue of customers for lemonade came to an end, and Katherine emerged from behind the table and headed for the food. Saham must have been waiting for this moment, for he shot up and marched alongside her. Reaching the table, she gathered a plateful of assorted victuals, hesitated for a moment, said something to Saham, and then walked over to the corner where Roger and Iris were settling themselves. I decided that the time had come for me to make a move. I nipped out of my seat, accelerated across the room and, by a quick zig-zag, slid into a chair almost under Saham's backside and exactly opposite to Katherine.

'Musical chairs later, old boy,' said Roger. 'And pardon me if I point out that you've slopped about half a pint of rot-gut on Tony's trousers. I should sponge them down at once, Tony old man, or you'll have a holy leg in about thirty seconds, if the colour of the brew is anything to go by. What in hell's name is it?'

'Lemonade,' I said, 'or so I was told.' And I glanced at Katherine for confirmation.

She nodded. 'Mrs Gorlestone's own recipe. Real lemon juice.'

'Squeezed herself over a pot, no doubt,' I said, unthinkingly.

'I say, old boy, ladies present,' said Roger. 'Well, whatever its origin, I'd pour it into the nearest aspidistra, if I were you. Stick to good old coffee.' And he drank deeply from his cup.

'Actually, it's not too bad,' I said, taking a tentative sip. 'And anyway, I expect the coffee's made from best acorns, or some foul herbal mixture.'

'As a matter of fact,' said Iris, 'it is. I don't know all that's in it, but she mentioned hawthorn, elder, succory, and viper's bugloss.'

'Good God!' said Roger, turning pale.

'Worried about the old digestion?' I asked, knowing that he was. 'Shall I fetch a stomach-pump?'

'William, darling, what a revolting idea!' said Iris.

'Oh, I don't know,' I said. 'We're due for some pretty gruesome entertainment already. I dare say most of the old ghouls would be thrilled to bits. It'd bring back happy memories of dear Miss Nightingale in the Crimea, and Dr Kildare, and other long-lost loved ones. It'd be the hit of the evening.'

'Well, if they're in the mood for black comedy, let's not stint them,' said Roger. 'A spot of vivisection might go down well. I'm sure there's one or two present who'd love to see the colour of your insides, Bill old man. Let's see. Old Shylock Gorlestone, no doubt, has got the best claim to wield the knife, but there are one or two others who might press her hard. You look distinctly uncooperative, old lad. What's up? Surely you'd do this little thing to please your beloved APES?'

'Butchered to make a simian holiday,' said Iris. 'I'm sure you'd be perfectly all right, William darling. And it would give Katherine a fabulous chance to demonstrate her remarkable kiss of life. Only do remember to wait until he's stopped breathing this time, Katherine dear.'

I looked sharply at Katherine. She was blushing like a shepherd's delight.

'These asparagus rolls are very nice,' I said, seeking to turn the conversation. 'Though no doubt someone will now tell me that it's not asparagus at all, it's the immature shoot of the lesser-spotted bugwort and terribly good for gravel and the stone. I wonder,' I added, thoughtfully, 'how she'll dispose of all the bodies?'

'Mr Oh-bwah!' said a well-known voice, a few inches abaft my right lug.

I sprang up, shooting an anchovy-pasted biscuit into the air. It fell to earth on Tony Saham's right shoulder, soft side down, and stuck, giving him momentarily a slight military look. He plucked it off with an exclamation.

'Sorry,' I said, holding out my plate. 'The anchovies must have been rather too fresh when they were pasted. Still, a fault on the right side.'

'Mr Oh-bwah,' said Mrs Gorlestone, heavily, 'I would like a word with you, if you find it convenient.'

We wandered off.

'I have been told, Mr Oh-bwah,' she said, when we had gone half-a-dozen steps, 'that you are musical.'

I'd expected to be accused of another frightful crime, and this took me rather by surprise.

'Oh, yes?' I said.

She took this, apparently, as agreement. 'We shall be starting the entertainment in a few minutes,' she said, 'and several people will be contributing songs.'

'Ah, well, yes,' I said, seeing where this was leading. 'But I can't sing for nuts.'

'That will not matter. I merely wish you to play the piano for the other singers. The fact is, Miss Bintry, who usually provides the accompaniment on these occasions, is a little unwell. I think she has been overcome by the heat.'

As a matter of fact, I had a shrewd idea of what had overcome Miss Bintry. Roger and I, coming down half an hour ago, had caught her on the first floor landing in the act of uncorking a silver-mounted flask.

'She does not feel able to play for us this evening,' continued Mrs Gorlestone, 'and there is no-one else with sufficient confidence to take her place. So I must ask you to do it. You will find all the necessary music on the lid of the instrument. Mr Gorlestone will turn the pages for you. He cannot read music, but he is quite used to conducting sing-songs with his boys. Richard,' she called, leading me over to the piano, 'I think it is time the entertainment began.'

And she buzzed off.

So the entertainment began, with R. Gorlestone as M.C., Patty Colkirk as cheerleader, and W. Hautbois as the poor pianist. As it happens I can sight-read fairly well, and there were some old favourites among the items. The main difficulty was estimating the singers' pace. There was some terribly in-and-out running. We started off with Cyril Thrigby, dreaming that he dwelt in marble halls. He loved those marble halls; we seemed to be in them for hours. Then Florence Babingley urged us to drink to her only with our eyes. This, fortunately, seemed to be all over in a matter of seconds. Mrs Gorlestone recited a Cautionary Tale, and Dick Gorlestone delivered a monologue to the ceiling. Ada Mulbarton, of Butt-like figure and thimbleful voice, gave us her vision of the Holy City; she was running out of breath as early as the end of the first verse, and the pace got slower and slower and the voice feebler and feebler as we crept towards the end. The third verse was practically a piano solo, with Mrs Mulbarton gamely miming the words. Patty Colkirk had a different technique. She started her eulogy of the Fishermen of England pretty slowly, but as breath got shorter she started to charge at the notes and by the middle of the second verse she was clearing several of them at a bound. Then Stan Hoe told a couple of funny stories; at least one presumed they were funny, for Elsie Cockthorpe laughed raucously at them, she being the only person in the audience who could penetrate the thick Yorkshire accent. The APES Glee Club then appeared, arranged itself neatly in two short ranks, and unfolded its music. At a wave from the paw of Cyril Thrigby the sopranos began that old favourite, 'Lavender's Blue', while the male voices roared in with 'It was a

Lover and his Lass'. This, apparently, was unplanned, for after a bar or two the sopranos began to nonny-no like the clappers, while the men, gallantly deciding that their duty was to rescue the ladies, heaved in a few hefty dilly-dillies. Then Mr Thrigby recounted his weird experience in a quaint old Cornish town, where he had done a spot of street-dancing accompanied by a curious nine-piece orchestra. This time, instead of dwelling, he went off at a furious pace, leaving me well behind. I stayed with him through most of the second verse, but he finished strongly, and at the post had his rather prominent nose well in front. Before I'd recovered my breath Stan Hoe thrust a tattered sheet of music on to the piano with a muttered injunction not to go too fast. It was handwritten, had no title, no words, and no tempo, and the key signature, which appeared only on the top stave, was partially obliterated by a dirty thumb-mark. I played the first few bars carefully, peering closely at it in an attempt to distinguish the accidentals from the fly-marks. It sounded like a dirge of some sort. Mr Hoe began to sing. His accent successfully concealed any meaning the words might have had, and in any case I was too occupied to listen. We kept pace reasonably well, but he seemed to have some difficulty in pitching the notes. After a while we came to the end of the verse, and a peculiar, sad little cadenza lifted us into the chorus.

'Yes, we have no - bananas,' sang Stan Hoe, full of remorse. 'We have no - bananas - today.'

The faulty key signature and the fly-blows had, between them, tricked me into playing it in the minor key.

After we'd staggered to the end Dick Gorlestone got up and announced that it was time for the high spot of the evening - Miss Overy's treasure-hunt. The rules were simple. We were to split into pairs, and each pair would be given a number and a written clue, which would direct them, etc. There would be a small prize for the first pair to reach the finishing line. Was that all clear?

From the expressions around him he gathered that it wasn't, so he explained it twice more. Then someone asked if the clues were all in the room, and he said no, they were mostly in the gardens and park. There was an immediate cackle of protest. The damp night air! My dear, I couldn't possibly... When the sheep had been sorted from the goats there appeared to be about twenty people who were willing to risk anything the evening vapours might do to them. I had a vague hope that I might, somehow, pair off with Katherine, but before I could make a move in her direction I found my way blocked by Mrs Gorlestone.

'Mr Oh-bwah,' she said, 'you will not, of course, take part in this treasure-hunt.'

'Well, as a matter of fact -'

'Many of our members,' she went on, ignoring my bleat, 'feel that they do not wish to go out again so late in the evening. They would rather stay here and enjoy some more entertainment. As Miss Bintry has not yet recovered from her indisposition we shall require your services as pianist.'

'Yes, but I was rather hoping that I could go -'

'Mr Oh-bwah, I must remind you that the School does not finish until tomorrow. Your first duty is towards the members of our association. I have no doubt, no doubt at all, that you would rather spend your time wandering about the park with some foolish gel or other, but that is not what we engaged you for.'

Well, I was about to say that I hadn't been engaged to play 'Yes, we have no bananas', either, but at that moment someone hailed her from the other end of the room, and, pausing only to indicate with an impatient gesture that my place was on the piano stool, she stumped off, leaving me dancing on the horns of a dilemma. Should I stay or should I choose freedom? At least I might run across Katherine and Saham in the park, for surely they'd be on the treasure hunt together. A quick glance told me that they were at the treasure hunt table. I chose freedom. As I passed through the French windows a fifteen-inch 'Oh-bwah!' burst against the jamb, but I didn't pause. Turning sharply to the right, I scampered along the terrace and found refuge in the formal garden.

It was a fine evening. The sun was almost down, but there was still plenty of light about, and after a while I decided to make my way to the lake. Apart from one or two fleeting glimpses of distant couples I'd seen nothing of the treasure-hunters, and I decided the lake and its surrounds might prove to be the focal point of the game. In fact, when I got there it seemed to be as deserted as the garden. The only thing of immediate interest was a small, classical boathouse, containing two rowing boats and a pair of canoes. I felt a sudden yearning for a life on the ocean wave. I chose the smaller of the rowing boats. It wasn't in the first bloom of youth, but I had no intention of doing a Kon-tiki.

The lake was a large one, shaped roughly like a well-filled sock, and about the position of the ankle-bone was a round, tree-covered island. I'd been wanting to investigate this island all week, for it was rumoured that there was some sort of building on it. I pondered for a short while. If I went to the island I should almost certainly forego any chance of meeting Katherine and Saham, while if I rowed about the lake I might well see them on the shore. But even if I saw them I could scarcely join them; and there was always the danger that Mrs Gorlestone might come looking for me, and on the lake I would be the easiest sort of sitting duck. So I decided to chuck everything and go to the island, and it wasn't long before I was tying the boat to a tree-root there.

It took me a little while to find the building, for the island was very overgrown. It wasn't as ruinous as I expected. There were a few bare rafters and the top of the chimney-stack had developed a dangerous list, but the walls were reasonably complete and the door still hung on its hinges. On the other hand, the shaggy thatch, the flaking plaster, and a pair of tiny pointed windows that were now mere sightless sockets gave it an undeniably sinister look, and it was with some little trepidation that I approached and pulled the door open. The first room that I came to was fitted with an early-nineteenth-century duck's nest grate with flanking cupboards and had obviously been the living-room. The second, leading off the first and sharing the front of the cottage, contained nothing but a nondescript fireplace and a mass of fallen plaster. The third, at the back of the living-room, was a backhouse-cum-larder, with wall oven and copper. However, what with the trees, the failing light, and the smallness of the windows, it was impossible to see much detail now, and I decided to come back tomorrow after the APES had gone and have another look at the place. The shades of night, in fact, were falling fast, and the *genius loci* was on the prowl, giving the edifice a distinctly creepy feeling. However, there was still a small door by the side of the copper to be investigated, so, reminding myself that I was in a simple Gothick cottage ornée and not the Castle of Otranto, I applied a tentative finger to the latch. It shot up with a report like a pistol. Startled, I paused, and it was in that moment that there came from the living-room a small, unearthly sound, somewhere between a grunt and a sigh.

I froze. For a moment you could have knocked chips off me with a hammer. Then the old Hautbois courage returned, and murmuring 'probably a hedgehog' I gave the door a yank. It scraped open a few inches, revealing the foot of a small flight of stairs. I was about to squeeze through the gap and ascend when a sixth sense told me that there was Something Strange behind me. I looked over my shoulder, and my blood stood on end. Framed in the doorway of the living-room was a tall, pale shape.

A sinister look

14

'Hello,' said the tall, pale shape, in the voice of Katherine Southwood.

'Woof!' I said, clinging to the doorpost. 'Stap me vitals! I thought you were the Great Mardle ghost.'

'Or a hedgehog?'

'Sorry. It was a most peculiar noise. And some of my best friends are hedgehogs.'

'We all get the friends we deserve. So this is where you come when the burden of the world is too much for you,' she went on, looking round with interest. 'What the agents would call an interesting property in a retired situation.'

'Full of Olde Worlde charm, but in need of some modernisation.' I was cheered by her willingness to converse. 'Have you seen the duck's-nest grate in the other room?'

We went back to the living-room and admired the grate. Then we found a piece of wattle-and-daub walling, and fell to discussing the possible age of the cottage. She seemed very knowledgeable. Absolutely wasted on Saham. And where the devil was he, anyway? Perhaps he was searching the island for clues in the treasure-hunt.

'I haven't seen them anywhere,' I said, following this thought.

'What?' she asked, with her head in a cupboard.

'The clues.'

'Oh. Well, there aren't any here, as a matter of fact. We thought it'd be tempting fate to have too many people rowing about on the lake.'

'You mean you helped with them? So you're not taking part in the actual hunt?'

'No.'

'In that case,' I asked, puzzled, 'why have you come to the island?'

'Well, if it comes to that, what are you doing here?'

'Oh, I'm a hunted man. Mrs Gorlestone sentenced me to spend the rest of the evening chained to the keyboard, so I took off. One of those now-or-never decisions. Was there much comment?'

'A fair bit. Mrs G. thought you ought to be skinned alive. But they'd all calmed down by the time I left. Roger was about to entertain them on the piano.'

'Then thank God I'm out here,' I said. 'What about you?'

'Oh, I'm on the run, too. Slimy Joe Bawdeswell. He started to make himself a little unpleasant, so I came out.'

'What about your - well, Tony Saham? Couldn't he see the old lecher off?'

'Well, actually, Tony wasn't in the room when I left.'

'Ah,' I said, thoughtfully, not knowing what to make of that. 'He must have got a shock when he found you'd gone.'

'I expect he'll survive.'

I braced myself to begin a tack towards the delicate subject of Iris. 'I suppose he's told you about his sensational discovery last night?'

She shut the cupboard door and turned away from it. 'Yes. Yes, he told me.'

'Well, I know it's a terrible old cliché, but I'd like you to hear my side of the story.'

'What makes you think I'd be in the least interested?'

'Well, there is that,' I admitted. 'But -'

'Ssssshh!' she said. 'Listen.'

We listened. A hollow, wooden sound was coming from no great distance.

'Rowlocks. Oars,' I added, hastily, in case she had misheard. 'Blasted treasure-hunters, I suppose.'

'Can't be.'

We gazed thoughtfully at each other. Presently the sounds of rowing were replaced by the sound of disembarkation.

'I'm not exactly keen on being found here,' I said. 'And I don't suppose you are either, in the circumstances.'

She shook her head, and went through to the back room. I followed, and opened the door to the stairs.

'Pretty grotty, isn't it?' she asked, peering over my shoulder.

'True. And that may be as well. I mean, I wouldn't think any casual visitors would risk their necks on it. What do you think?'

'Lead on.'

I began to ascend. She followed, shutting the door behind her. It was definitely murky, and the first thing I did when I reached the top was to put a foot through a hole in the floorboards. A great shower of plaster fell into the room beneath, but I managed to cling to the shaky banister-rail.

'Are you all right?' she asked, coming up close behind me.

'Yes, thanks. Mind the rotten boards. Anyone in sight yet?'

We were standing at the head of the stairs on one side of the room. A small dormer window gave a rather limited view of the little jungle that had been the front garden. The newcomers were crashing through the undergrowth from the boathouse side of the island, so there was a good chance that they hadn't seen my boat, which was tied up on the far side. Presently they emerged from the gloom.

'Crumbs,' murmured Katherine. 'The fuzz.'

It was Dr Subcourse and Mrs Gorlestone.

We looked down at the stair door, and then at each other. If anyone peered up the stairs they'd be sure to see us. The room we were in contained nothing but a broken-down iron bedstead and an unsavoury heap of decayed sacks. With a common impulse we tiptoed across the grimy floor to the other bedroom. This was even barer than the first, and the only feature was a small door under the slope of the roof by the chimney-breast. I eased it open and peered in, half expecting to find a partially dismembered corpse. It was a shallow cupboard, wedge-shaped, with a maximum height at the chimney-breast of about three feet. We looked at it without enthusiasm.

'There's nowhere else,' she whispered. 'In you go.'

I crept in and arranged myself at length against the back wall. She crushed in after me, sitting partly on my legs and partly on the floor. I never even thought of complaining.

We'd only just closed the door when voices told us that the enemy was beneath. The floorboards were full of cracks, and we could hear every word.

'Mr Oh-bwah! Miss Southwood!' called Mrs Gorlestone.

'H'm. No answer,' said the doctor, after a pause.

'My dear doctor, one would scarcely expect them to answer.'

The dear doctor restrained himself from demanding why the hell she'd called out.

'He - was - sure - they - came - to - the - island?' he asked. Each word was followed by a suck, so I knew his pipe was not going well.

'He said they came in this direction,' Mrs Gorlestone answered. 'I do not think that he would attempt to mislead me, particularly as there seems to be some personal feeling between them. He seems a thoroughly reliable young man. I'm sure you have made the right decision, doctor.'

'Thank you.'

'However, that is not our concern at the moment. We must search the cottage. This is just the sort of place they would choose.'

'Quite,' said the doctor, striking a match and sucking hard.

'We must search everywhere. Everywhere. Every nook and cranny. What is in that cupboard?'

The door of the cupboard downstairs creaked open.

'Nothing. Nothing,' said the doctor.

'We cannot afford to leave the smallest space unsearched. I am determined to find it and confront them with it.'

'The corset,' whispered Katherine.

I nodded. As it was pitch black the gesture was useless, but her hair brushed pleasantly against my chin.

The search party began to move about downstairs. The door of the oven squeaked, indicating that they were in the backhouse. Then the stair door scraped open.

'Mr Oh-bwah! Miss Southwood!' Funnelled up the stair, Mrs Gorlestone's voice sounded like the Doomsday call to judgement. 'Are you there, Miss Southwood?'

I felt Katherine giggling, and so did the cupboard, for a piece of plaster scuttered to the floor.

'I heard a noise,' said Mrs Gorlestone. 'Doctor, you must investigate.'

I don't think the doctor was too keen, as there was a long pause before the stairs began to creak. As he reached the top there was the noise of falling plaster and a muttered, but no doubt academic, oath.

'I can see nothing here,' he called. 'But there is another room. I'll see if I can get to it.'

'This is it,' whispered Katherine. 'Can we jam the door somehow?'

I swept my hand over the inside of the door and found a small coathook. I grasped it, and Katherine's hand closed over mine.

'Ah, a cupboard.' The doctor's voice was very close. We braced ourselves. The knob rattled. 'Stuck!' he muttered, and gave it a yank that nearly took my finger off. The door yammered but remained shut, and Katherine let out an involuntary squeak.

'Rats!' exclaimed the doctor.

Katherine squeaked again. Following her lead, I did a delicate little scrabble on the boards with the fingers of my other hand.

The doctor let go of the knob and stepped back. There was a creak, followed immediately by a splintering crash and a sort of scuttering thud from below. The doctor had taken the short way down.

'Doctor! Are you hurt?' cried Mrs Gorlestone, hurrying through to the living-room beneath us.

'I don't think so. No. No. Shaken, but not - *hurt.* Fortunately my fall was partially broken by this straw. Thank you, my dear Mrs Gorlestone, I am quite able to stand. I don't think we need to linger here. Those thoughtless young people are evidently not here. I propose that we make our way back to the house. Perhaps we could resume our search in the morning, when there is more light.'

Mrs Gorlestone, reluctantly, agreed. The outer door squeaked open and slammed.

'They've gone,' murmured Katherine, taking her hand away from the hook.

'So they have.' I put one hand lightly on her shoulder. She remained perfectly still. After a few breathless moments I touched her neck; still she did not move, so I began to stroke her, very gently, just beneath the right ear. Her hand came up and her fingers lay lightly on mine. As I bent my head towards her I caught, in the corner of my eye, a glimpse of a wavering, reddish glow through a gap in the floorboards. Reluctantly I peered at it; then I sat up with a jerk, catching my forehead a stunner on the common purlin.

'Bloody hell!' I said. 'Sorry, but I think the house is on fire.'

We scrambled out of the cupboard and pelted down the stairs. By the time we got to the living-room the straw was going well, and our way to the door was blocked. Flames were beginning to run up the woodwork of the fireside cupboard, and a few sparks were glowing on the bare boards of the floor above. We turned to the backhouse. A couple of shoulder-charges burst open the decrepit door. The back garden was a head-high jungle, but we managed to fight our way through to the safety of the trees. As we turned to look at the cottage, now going extremely well, two dim figures emerged from the shadows on the far side. We ducked down and crept into the bushes, and a few minutes later found ourselves at the water's edge. My boat was still there, and tied up alongside was a canoe.

'Yours?' I asked.

'Yes. Shall we go?'

'I suppose we'd better,' I said, strangely reluctant to leave the island. 'Can I give you a lift home?'

'What about my canoe?'

'We can hitch it on behind.'

We did so, and embarked. I took the oars and headed out into the lake. When we were a little distance from the island I rested on the oars. Sparks were shooting high above the trees and flames were glowing through the undergrowth.

'It's really rather a splendid sight, isn't it?' she said. 'And yet - well, it's a pity.'

'Yes. Mind you, it could have been a bit draughty in the winter. Are you warm enough, or would you like to move closer to the fire?'

She laughed. 'I'm all right. Look, there goes the old *Walrus.*'

A boat, with Dr Subcourse at the oars and coxed by Mrs Gorlestone, left the other side of the island. After half-a-dozen strokes he rested and looked up.

'Dammit, he's seen us,' I said. The doctor was clearly pointing us out to Captain Flint, and after a short council of war they headed towards us.

'Sail ho!' called Katherine, not too softly. 'Hello,' she added, as soon as she could see the whites of their eyes. 'What a nice evening, Dr Subcourse. I *did* enjoy the entertainment, but I hadn't realised there was to be a bonfire as well. Will there be fireworks?'

'Miss Southwood! Where have you been?' demanded Mrs Gorlestone.

'Oh, just paddling about. I met Mr Hautbois over there -' she gestured vaguely towards the end of the lake - 'and he offered me a lift, as my canoe was a little damp.'

Mrs Gorlestone brought her stern gun to bear as the doctor allowed his boat to swing round. 'Mr Oh-bwah, where have you been? Have you been to the island?'

'I've been *round* it,' I said, carefully. 'It looks a bit overgrown. I've heard there's some sort of Gothicky building on it. Good lord! Don't say it's on fire! I've been hoping to visit it all week. Bother!'

'Mr Oh-bwah! What have you been doing since you ran from the room?'

It was my turn to wave a vague hand. 'Oh, I've been here and there, you know, trying to be helpful to the treasure-hunters. And Miss Southwood's canoe was getting a bit waterlogged, so I offered her a lift. We were just heading for the shore when we saw the fire. I say, it *is* going well. Do you think we're safe here?' I asked, as a cloud of sparks swirled up into the sky.

'Perfectly safe,' said the doctor, who had rested his oars and was now patting his pockets. There was a thoughtful look on his face. 'I think, Mr Hautbois, that we shall require a more detailed - a much more detailed - account of your movements, and those of Miss Southwood, before we can accept your explanation.'

'Doesn't it smell nice!' said Katherine, enthusiastically. 'There must be some rare and special herb burning. I thought at first it was your pipe, Dr Subcourse, but I can see now that you're not smoking it. I hope you haven't *lost* it somewhere?'

The doctor was still searching his pockets. 'Ah - I seem - ah - to have mislaid it,' he said. 'Now I wonder where - h'm. Yes. I had it in my mouth when I was in… good God!'

We all followed his gaze. The fire seemed to be going better than ever.

'Ah - what a pleasant evening for a little - ah - boating,' he said, turning back to us. One corner of his mouth writhed unpleasantly, and it took me some moments to realise that it was an unpractised attempt at a conciliatory smile. 'Of course, it may have appeared that we - ah - came from the island, but, well

- ha-ha - appearances can be deceptive, as I'm sure you realise. But perhaps - in the circumstances - ha-ha - it would be as well if you didn't mention -'

'Doctor!' cut in Mrs Gorlestone. 'I think it is time we returned to the house. I am sure that Miss Southwood and Mr Oh-bwah will not spread any unfounded rumours. Mr Oh-bwah, it will not be necessary for you to accompany us. No doubt you have much to discuss. Come, doctor.'

The doctor bent to the oars, and in a minute or two they were hull down on the horizon.

'Drive on, James,' said Katherine, leaning back.

'Where to, madam?'

'Oh, anywhere. It's far too nice an evening to waste.'

I began to paddle round the island in an incredulous daze, moving the oars gingerly in case I caught a crab and woke up. Had I psyched myself into a sort of Spenserian fantasy? Or was I in some department of Paradise - burnt to a crisp in the fire, and now drifting through eternity in a cut-price Arthurian barge? In either case, Katherine was likely to vanish at a touch. Reality was even worse. This was the last evening, and I wouldn't see her again, unless I got an invitation to the wedding. And that was neither likely nor desirable. I sighed.

'You look rather lubricious,' she said.

'Eh?' I said, startled.

'No, no, I don't mean that. Lub - lib - what's the word?'

'Libidinous? Lecherous? Lascivious?'

'No. Lub - lugubrious, that's it.'

'Ah. A Freudian slip, no doubt.'

'Oh, no doubt,' she said, easily. 'Your reputation, you know...'

'Undeserved,' I said, gloomily. 'I suppose you're thinking about last night?'

'Among other things. It does add up. First there was the pink nightdress,' she said, ticking it off on a finger, 'Then the rape of the corset. Then the dressing-gown in the wardrobe. And last night the great discovery of the close embrace, as reported by Our Own Correspondent.'

'Ah, well, that was not quite what it appeared to be. You see -'

'Don't tell me she fainted, and you were just supporting her till help arrived?'

'Well, not -'

'Or perhaps you were treating her lumbago by the tried and tested Valentino method?'

'No. Look, what he saw was simply - well, just -'

'A teeny little thank-you kiss.'

'That's right, a teeny - how the deuce do you know that?'

'Intuition. No, actually Iris came and made a clean breast of everything last night.'

'Did she! I mean, everything?'

'Well, she *said* it was everything. She rather cast herself in the role of the classic temptress - you know, a sort of blend of Delilah, Cleopatra, and Mrs Simpson. Only a man with an iron will such as yours could have resisted her.'

'She said *that?'*

'Well, not in so many words. In fact, she said you didn't seem to be able to put your heart into it. Something seemed to be holding you back - a nonconformist conscience, or a sweet little wife back home, or something.'

'Good lord, no - that is, well, there was, of course. Not a wife.'

'Oh, *not* a wife?'

'No. Just a passing thought. A sort of *déjà vu,* really,' I said, editing hurriedly. 'Oft in the Stilly Night. Moore. Thomas Moore,' I added quickly, to avoid further misunderstanding, 'and Ruskin. Only in my case it wasn't a song that awakened the conscience. More like an owl, a cat, and Rothschild's Grackles. But what I don't understand is why Iris felt she had to tell you.'

'No, neither do I,' she murmured, tracing an Hogarthian line of beauty on the surface of the water. 'Ah, well. The moving finger writes, and having writ - well. Look, there's the moon.'

It was awkwardly placed abaft my left shoulder. I began to turn the boat, then had a better idea.

'So it is,' I agreed. The boat wobbled slightly as I sat down beside her. 'Ah, Moon of my Delights who know'st no wane, the Moon of Heav'n is rising once again -'

'How oft hereafter rising shall she look Through this same Garden after me - in vain,' she said, softly completing the quatrain.

'Yes, that's it.'

'What's the matter?'

'You are. I suppose I could forbid the banns,' I went on, trying to speak lightly. Every word was stamped out of lead. 'It'd look well in the *Borshire Chronicle.* "There was a disturbance yesterday in Brattling church at the publication of the banns of marriage, between Miss Katherine Southwood, daughter of Lord Brattling, and Mr Anthony Saham. A shabbily-dressed man interrupted the Revd Henry Pooter (58) by climbing on to a pew and shouting abusively that it was all wrong. He was removed by the churchwardens. Interviewed later, the man, who refused to give his name, said there were two very just causes and one extremely heavy impediment, namely an owl, a cat, and a horsehair sofa. He accompanied police to the nearest police-station, where he is helping them with their inquiries into cases of wilful damage and arson." I suppose if he turned up at the altar in that jazzy sweater the parson might refuse to perform. And yet I don't know; the clergy are notoriously lax these days.'

'I'm sorry. I should have told you before.' She didn't sound at all contrite, but then, why should she?

'It doesn't matter. I'd have fallen for you anyway. Well, that's life. I suppose I shall have to go to the South Seas and shoot copra.'

'Oh, I always thought copra was a fish.' She swirled her finger in the water again. 'But what I really meant was -'

'Katherine.'

'Yes?'

I put a tentative arm round her shoulders. I half expected her to squirm away, but she didn't. She leant back slightly. Her eyes seemed to be unusually large, and her lips were parted slightly. In for a penny, I bent and kissed her. The boat swayed gently. This *must* be paradise.

'Dear me,' she murmured, when at length we drew apart. 'What a surprise!'

'I'm sorry,' I said, hopelessly.

'You ought to be ashamed of yourself, taking advantage of a poor girl's *mal-de-mer*. But I didn't mean... listen. You remember when Mrs Gorlestone more or less accused us of sharing a bed?'

'Yes,' I said, wondering what was coming.

'Well, it was an emergency, wasn't it?'

'Yes,' I said, still fogged.

'Well, I had to fish some sort of spectacular rabbit out of the hat. So I told her that there couldn't be anything between *us*, because I was engaged to Tony. I never dreamt that *everyone* would believe it.'

'What!'

'I just made it up, on the spur of the moment. I thought you knew that - at least, I did until Iris came to see me last night. Of course, I didn't reckon on the old dragon - Mrs Gorlestone, I mean - going off to Tony later that afternoon to check up on the story. And then he got very stupid about it. I suppose I can't blame him, when he had it from such a horsey mouth. That'll teach me to be economical with the truth. I've had to spend practically all day fighting him off, when I could have - well. I didn't finally convince him till this evening.'

'How?' I asked, still slightly concussed by these revelations.

'Oh, well - no, no, I'm not going to tell you. You might think - well -'

'I might indeed,' I said, edging a little closer and slipping a noticeably less tentative arm around her. 'Do you realise, young Southwood, the anguish you've caused by not telling me sooner? I might have been scarred for life.'

'Nonsense. You didn't care a bit. If Tony hadn't blundered in you'd have gathered rosebuds by the bucketful. Anyway, I could hardly come up to you and say "By the way, I'm not engaged to Tony Saham," could I? I mean, it would have sounded much too like an invitation, wouldn't it?'

'Much too much,' I said, drawing her to me.

Some minutes later we became aware of the gentle plash of oars. It was Roger and Iris in the *Walrus*.

'Hullo hullo hullo! What's all this, then? River police here,' said Roger, as they drew alongside.

'William, what have you and Katherine been doing?' asked Iris, making a large gesture at the fire. 'Don't tell me your smouldering passions have blazed up at last? Katherine dear, you look quite flushed.'

'None of our doing,' I said. 'The fire, I mean. The doctor and Mrs Gorlestone were searching for the Golden Corset, and somehow he managed to drop his pipe and ignite a perfectly good Gothick cottage. We saw it all - from a safe distance. Came in quite useful when they tried to interrogate us. Anyway, a spectacular end to a spectacular week. How's the party?'

'Dead as mutton,' said Roger.

'How come? I thought you were doing your world-famous Schnozzle Durante act. Surely no party could die after that?'

'Schnozzle schmozzle. Even Durante would have been a bit too recent for them. I'd have done better with a quick impression of Little Tich, or even dear Mr Garrick. In fact, I was sorely tempted to bring Humphrey Godwick back to life, if only to make Subcourse and his moll look a couple of pratts.'

'Tut, tut! You seem upset. What's the matter?'

'Words fail me. Tell them, Iris.'

'William, dear,' said Iris, 'Bad news, I'm afraid. Tony Saham's got the job.'

'So that's who they were talking about in the cottage,' I said. 'Well, good luck to him, I say. After this week, I don't fancy spending the next few years under the Subcourse heel. Anyway, after Wednesday I knew I didn't stand a cat's chance. I thought Roger might have got it, though.'

'So did I,' said Roger. 'Ah, what the hell. Something'll turn up. Anyway, I've got a consolation prize.' He squeezed Iris.

'That's a sexist way of putting it,' said Katherine. 'But talking of prizes, who won the treasure-hunt?'

'Dick Gorlestone and his Patty,' said Roger. 'I laughed like a drain. Brilliant idea of yours, young Katherine. You should have seen their faces when they opened it.'

'Why, what was it?' I asked.

'The notorious corset. Wrapped up and posing as half a hundredweight of crappy health-food. All the work of our fair companions.'

'Katherine did the actual switch in Mr Gorlestone's room,' said Iris. 'In *such* a professional way, too. One would have thought she's used to slipping in and out of scoutmasters' bedrooms. I should keep an eye on her, William, or she'll be off with the next Brown Owl or whatever it is.'

'Barn owl, actually,' said Katherine. 'Though I really prefer Rothschild's grackles.'

'I don't understand that, Katherine dear. Roger, darling, shall we look at the fire from the other side, where it's less crowded? See you later, my pets. Be good.'

'And you,' said Katherine. 'Mind you don't upset the boat.'

As they passed round the edge of the island we became aware of a distant braying. Far up the slope of the park appeared the local fire-engine. It tore down to the shore of the lake, braked sharply, skidded, paused briefly, did a savage U-turn with an angry snarl of gears, and roared back up the slope. Evidently no-one had thought to mention that the fire was on the island. As it passed the end of Great Mardle Hall it gave a final derisive blast and vanished into the dusk.

'How peaceful it all is,' said Katherine.

Great Mardle Hall